One Summer

One Summer

Jim Ellis

Acknowledgements

Thanks to Cynthia Weiner, Libby Jacobs, and Miriam Santana for their support and encouragement; and a warm thank you to Maggie McClure for proof reading. A special thank you to my Good Lady, Jeannette.

To see her is to love her,
And love but her for ever;
For nature made her what she is,
And ne'er made such anither

Robert Burns, Bonnie Leslie

Chapter One

Nathan Forrest lived in Westburn, a town built by the river, its fading glories sprung from shipbuilding and marine engineering, many of its 80,000 souls sustained by stoicism and God's Mercy. The workers were crammed into tenements and drab estates on the edges of the town; the better off enjoyed a spacious suburb to the west. The working people felt compensated by the beauty of the river and the views of the mountains. The middle classes took it all for granted.

Nathan saw only High Summer in Westburn, and was blind to winter coming. In 1958 orders replacing wartime losses had dried up, but the yards held on, building new ships.

When he left the Army, Nathan had mastered welding and now worked on the submarines building for the Royal Navy. Had he lifted his eyes he might have seen that this way of life was mouldering. But Nathan made good money and did not worry that class solidarity was dying, and management control of the business of shipbuilding was slipping.

The yard managers knew how to build ships, but they hadn't a clue about leadership and had no respect for the men. At ten o'clock every morning, they sat in warm offices, drinking tea and nibbling biscuits served on Company china by liveried tea ladies from the Management Restaurant; the staff obtained refreshments from the Staff Canteen. The men took an unofficial break, hiding in draughty corners of part-built hulls and steel fabrications, sneaking a bite of egg roll, slurping hot, sweet tea from a thermos flask or a tea can. Sometimes the men's meal was disrupted when an aggressive young manager, or an old management hard case feeling his oats, raided the hiding places, chasing the men back to work.

One Thursday, a senior manager, an old warhorse, ambushed a tea boy brewing up for his squad and booted the tin tea cans to the ground, trampling them underfoot. The boy, cowering from the manager's rage, tripped on an upturned tea can and fell. It looked as if the manager had pushed the boy to the ground, and Nathan was outraged when the boy got sacked. The fury of the men erupted in a wildcat strike, emptying the yard in twenty minutes. Nathan joining the hate-filled throng milling at the yard gate, refusing to disperse until management summoned the police.

The following Monday, management's stomach for the fight collapsed and the Tea Boy Strike ended when the manager apologized and the boy was reinstated.

But sometimes the unions sank low. A young manager saw a workman defecating inside a steel fabrication and dismissed him. Nathan was sickened by the man's filthy habits and agreed with the firing, but he doubted the judgement of the Unions, when the shop stewards fought and had the miscreant reinstated. Nathan retreated again from life in the yard and backed farther into his private world.

Some of Nathan's friends went abroad, but Nathan was impervious to the creeping rot killing the yard: the struggles of management and unions, and the ending of the old way of life. He turned aside from the decay surrounding him; Nathan was content and did not want to shift overseas, and have to deal with changes to his trade, and the way he lived. He was an elite welder earning good money, supporting what really mattered to him: his life outside the yard as a Jazz musician. It would have been better for Nathan were the yards to implode through sudden, unexpected crisis, driving him out of his crumbling niche, opening his eyes to the truths of his situation. Nathan was far from stupid and could have worked out the uncertainties and difficulties lying ahead; but he was indifferent to the struggles for respect; and heedless of the slow death rattle rising from shipbuilding and his people.

Nathan wrapped himself in a comforting blanket of tolerable wages and his other life in Jazz. It would take a great storm to set Nathan free.

Nathan was twenty-five of lean build and stood at five-foot ten inches. He dressed in sober, dark wool jackets and slacks. The cut was hip. Hip for Westburn and working class: drape jackets with sack back and narrow pants and well-polished loafers. He liked soft, solid coloured shirts and wool ties. With his dark hair cut short and neatly parted, he came close to the look favoured by some American Jazz musicians he'd seen at concerts in Glasgow.

That Friday, with the working week over, Nathan walked out the yard gate with Leo, an alto saxophone player and co-leader of the band. He offered to pick up Nathan and drive him to the Friday night gig, but Nathan preferred to walk.

Later that evening, Nathan went down the four stairs leading from the main door of the terraced house where he lived, looked across rooftops and through tall chimneys, free of smoke so close to mid summer. Nathan's eyes rested on the masts and funnels of vessels in the harbour, then moved on to the silhouettes of ships anchored in the river. He paused outside the house for a minute, taking in the views of the cranes; tall, sinister skeletons perched over the frames and hulls of part built vessels. And below them, invisible from the heights of Galt Place was the sub, a black, deep-sea creature, cramped and packed with weapons and machinery. He hated all of it; was sick of the hard drinking and coarsened lives that went with it and yet, grudgingly, Nathan admired the innovation and industry that created it. Perversely, he was proud of the ships that his people, the working class, built there.

Nathan and Leo were welders on the sub and would be back inside its confined spaces on Monday morning, bulky in pigskin jackets and gauntlets, the moleskin trousers: all this kit to protect them from burns; and the heavy boots with steel toe caps. Nathan seldom lost the feel of the tight beret on his head and the welding hood that fitted snugly over it. Monday to Friday, he stared through the dark window of the hood at the blue arc of the burning welding rod.

Nathan headed west to the affluent suburb and Westburn Rugby Club. At the end of Galt Place he turned to let his eyes linger on the full sweep of the small terraced villas and the house where he lived with Ma. Galt Place was elegant when built early in the 19th Century.

Now, carelessness and neglect enveloped Galt Place. Year by year, ruin gained. Peeling paint, crumbling stonework, stained windows, shabby entrances and stairs assaulted his eyes. But the quality of Victorian craftsmanship survived in the elegant bay windows, the deep eaves, ornate sofit boards and solid, hardwood doors.

Ma cared for their house, keeping paintwork and fitments neat and clean. She struggled against the indifference and despair of her neighbours. Nathan often wondered how long Ma and he could hold back the flood tide of decay.

Nathan liked walking through Westburn on the way to a gig, the Bach trumpet safe in its case tucked under his arm. He walked down the steep hill of Ann Street and entered The Square, past the old Empire Theatre, shabby now that it was closed and abandoned. There was no theatre, no variety shows or musicals in Westburn and had Nathan read the signs on billboards and in the local newspaper, he might have predicted that his great passion, Jazz, would struggle to be heard, as amateur folk groups mushroomed in popularity capturing gigs from musicians like himself. Had he looked closely he might have noticed that some venues for young people already preferred record hops to live musicians. He stared for a minute at the regal Municipal Buildings, raising his head to see the top of the Royal Tower soaring above.

Walking westwards, Nathan crossed the Great Divide of Westburn: Lord Nelson Street, lined with the symbols of authority: the Sheriff Court, the Grammar School, the established Protestant churches and in particular, the Town Kirk and its clock chiming the quarter hours, reminding Nathan's people that they did not belong west of this line. These buildings like Forts on Hadrian's Wall, a deterrent to entry by working class barbarians into middle class Valentia.

Nathan turned towards the river passing his old school that he habitually referred to as 'The Borstal for Retarded Tims.' His time there ended on a sour note when the School Chaplain, Father Brendan Toner, a cruel Irishman humiliated him in front of the class. It was a about a week before he was due to leave. Nathan was fourteen.

"Are you Catholic boy?" the Chaplain said.

"Yes, Father."

"Are your parents Catholic?"

"Ma mother wis. She's dead. Ma father's dead. Ah don't know if he wis a Catholic."

Behind him, Nathan heard the titters of the class.

"And were they married?"

Nathan felt the swelling in his throat and tears coming. He didn't answer.

"Who brought you up, boy?"

"Ma did."

"And tell me boy, who is Ma; is she Catholic?"

Nathan fought back the tears, silently cursing the brute. The class was laughing now.

"Ma's ma Grandmother."

"Ah," the priest sighed. "Born out of wedlock. Why in Ireland, boy, a good Catholic family would've taken you in and fostered you."

Cold rage took hold of Nathan; he'd had enough. "Ma an' me, we're a good Catholic family."

The priest cuffed Nathan, hard and he staggered from the force of the blow. "Do not speak back to me, boy"

Nathan ran for the door, turning as he opened it. "Ya fuckin' ol' cunt," he shouted.

He never went back to school and he finished with the Catholic Church.

The walk on the Esplanade by the river and the views of the mountains to the northwest banished the memories of the Irish priest. Nathan was a lone raider walking in the West End. He imagined the residents preferred that people like him, working class and Catholic, stay away. They were happy enough tolerating the tradesmen and the cleaning women who worked in the houses; and they did not mind too much the deliverymen bringing goods. Nathan liked to think of the consternation the residents of the West End might feel of a Sunday afternoon when his people came in large numbers, dressed in their Sunday best, family groups and friends walking and having a good look.

He laughed imagining the residents' sense of relief when the working classes began their slow retreat on a Sunday evening to the crowded enclaves of tenements and the new estates established at the frontier of Westburn.

The vibrating chords of the bass and swish of rhythm brushes faded; the melody of Tenderly stayed with Nathan for a few moments as the last couples left the dance floor.

"Thank Christ it's over," he said.

He hated that gig, Westburn Rugby Club's Summer Ball. He'd heard that Catholics were barred, but as he'd given up his Faith and didn't like rugby, so what?

What Nathan loathed was the boorish behaviour of the members; they ignored Nathan and Leo, and the other members of the band: the hired help brought in for their entertainment. And he did not like the snobby, aloof women: big, horsy bints, all bum and tits.

The Club had once been a grand Victorian residence; its rooms beautifully proportioned, retaining many of the original features, a sweeping staircase leading to the upper floor. Nathan could not help but admire the style and elegance of the place.

Nathan returned from the lavatory, glancing into the bar where two of the hearties lay, passed out. One of them, Eric, had pissed into his cavalry twills. Nathan was glad it was Eric; a perfect shit. There was a pool of vomit soaking into the seat of the chair where his head rested at an awkward angle.

Earlier, Eric, dandified in an English cut Donegal tweed jacket and striped Club tie, drunk and querulous, but still on his feet, had demanded the band play Scottish Country-dances.

"We don't do Scottish Country-dances," Nathan said.

Eric worked at the yard, a ship's draughtsman. Once, Nathan had pointed out an error in one of his drawings. The weld was in the wrong place. Eric hated that.

"I'm speaking to you," Eric said, nodding at Leo.

Leo pointed to Nathan, "We lead the band. Like he said, we don't do Scottish Country-Dances."

"This is ridiculous" Eric said. "You're being paid to entertain us."

"Ah tell ye, Mate," Leo said. "We'll leave right now, an' ye can shove yer money up yer arse."

Nathan opened the valve on the Bach and let the accumulated spit drain on to the floor; Eric swayed back. "So, what's it to be?"

"Damned common riff raff," Eric muttered, staggering away.

Nathan removed the mute, and then dried off the Bach trumpet. Leo had his Conn alto in the case, Chuck covered the bass and Joe finished packing the drum kit.

"Let's go, Nathan," Leo said.

Chuck and Joe were outside putting the bass and drums into the back of Leo's beat up Humber estate car.

"No' bad for this fuckin' place," Nathan said to Leo as they walked to the main door of the club. He looked in the bar again. Eric and the other hearty still lay there, passed out. "Gentlemen, eh?"

"Money's good, Nathan. Don't knock it."

"Fuckin' tossers."

When they got to the door, it was raining steadily on an ambulance parked at the gate. The ambulance men passed a stretcher with a body lying on it, into the back.

Dorothy Jones, the kid he'd met earlier stood at the door. Nathan liked the way her white dirndl skirt hung below mid calf, a pretty white border for her coat. He and Leo stopped; not relishing a sprint through the rain to the car, hoping Chuck had the wit to bring the car over to the door once the ambulance had gone.

Dorothy had come up to the band at the interval, just as they'd finished playing a hard driving rendering of Wives and Lovers. She held out her hand,

"I'm Dorothy Jones. That was a lovely and an exciting song. What's it called?"

She was a sweet girl. Her pretty lilac blouse and flat summer shoes went well with the white dirndl skirt. Some people might see Dorothy flawed by slightly prominent teeth. Nathan liked her pale complexion and well cut, short fair hair. He pressed her hand and he thought that one of the bears had taste, inviting her to the Ball.

"Hello, Dorothy. Thanks. It's called Wives and Lovers, written by Hal David and Burt Bacharach. I'm Nathan," he said, and pointing to the band, "Leo, Chuck, Joe, meet Dorothy." They waved and she smiled.

Leo and Nathan had a passion for Hal David, and Burt Bacharach songs. They'd swung into Wives and Lovers, coaxing and driving each other to sharp, jangling improvisations. They brought Chuck and Joe to playing sensed, swinging rhythms.

Many of the rugby men, too far gone in drink to notice the shift to Jazz, as they shuffled round, out of step, heavy brogues bruising their partners feet.

Nathan saw Leo's beat up Humber estate approaching the gate. "Something wrong, Dorothy?" he said.

"Oh, hello. Charles, the boy who brought me, was up to high jinks and broke his leg when he fell down the stairs. I think he was drunk. His friends are away with him to the hospital."

Back in the recesses of the Club the rear guard of the revelers burst into a raw chorus, attempting to resuscitate the corpse of the Ball.

"Mary from the Mountain Glen,
Fucked herself with a fountain pen…
They called the Bastard, Stephen; they called the Bastard Stephen,
For that was the name of the blue-black ink."

He felt for Dorothy having to listen to this and he quivered with fury at their unthinking use of bastard.

"Are you going home?"

"Yes, I'm going to walk."

It was after one and raining hard. She was in for a soaking in her light summer coat. She'd be going by a quiet road to a pleasant middle class street, but there might be trouble with a stray drunk on the way.

Nathan turned to Leo. "Leo, got room for one more?

"Sure, as long as you don't mind the instruments, Miss."

Joe and Chuck wanted dropped off first and Nathan and Leo chatted to Dorothy Jones as they drove them home.

"Don't you have a Jazz Club where you play, or do you just play at dances?" Dorothy said.

Leo caught Nathan's eye in the rear view mirror and they both laughed.

"Yes, we have a place," Nathan said. "It's not much, but sometimes the music is pretty good."

Their Jazz sanctuary: primitive with inadequate heating and a dire toilet. Nathan and Leo paid to have the battered upright piano tuned and they played and heard some great jazz there on Sunday nights. It attracted riff raff with nothing to do on Sunday evenings. The room was located behind and above a tacky fish and chip restaurant, rumoured to be a brothel. The Palm Grove. They called it Greasy Bella's. Regularly, foreign seamen came and went through its portal. The owner of The Palm Grove let the room for a nominal fee. The fans attracted to a Sunday night gig consumed large quantities of his fish and chips at the interval and when they'd finished.

Westburn, 1958; there were few restaurants and none opened at night. Dining out in the evening, generally meant eating on the hoof, standing in shop doorways or sitting on a park bench in fine weather, hands moving rapidly in and out of paper parcels loaded with salty, soggy, vinegary fish and chips. Nathan hated the smell of cold fat and vinegar lingering on his hands and fingers.

"I don't think you'd like it much, Miss," Leo said.

"Why not? And please call me Dorothy. I hate being called, Miss."

Leo pulled a face in the rear view mirror. "Sorry."

"That's Calle Crescent. Can you stop at sixteen?"

Leo pulled over. Nathan got out, mounted the pavement and let Dorothy Jones out of the car. "Come on, I'll see you to the door."

"Thank you."

He held the gate open and followed her up the path to the front door. It burst open filling the entrance with light and then, the bulky shape of a big man darkened the light.

"Dorothy. What do you mean coming in at this hour? Who is this man?"

"This is Nathan; he helped me and gave me a lift home. He plays in the band."

"Band is it? Damned hooligans. You, get to hell out of here."

He moved towards his daughter, raising his arm to strike her and Nathan stood between them. Nathan choked on the stink of whisky. Dorothy cowered. Nathan saw his face, Jones, the senior manager in charge of submarine building down the yard.

He was a brutal big man. The men called him Horse Jones, after the Hoss character in the TV Western, Bonanza.

Nathan never took on fights since leaving the Army. He worried about injuries to hands, lips and front teeth. Broken fingers, split lips and a wrecked embrasure that he'd spent years shaping and toughening. Fatal for a trumpet player: but he'd not walk away from this man.

"There's no need for that," Nathan said, raising his hands, palms out, offering Horse Jones peace or a square go.

Nathan had a deep sense of chivalry towards women that went beyond respect and admiration. He despised Horse Jones for his drunkenness and the violence he wanted to wreak on Dorothy.

He wanted to see this girl again, but he knew that if he didn't protect her, he never would. Nathan caught Dorothy's elbow and steered her towards the door. Her arm trembled. "Go on, get inside and into bed. We'll fix this up. Don't worry."

Leo's squat solid figure was between Horse Jones and Nathan. "You're right out o' order, Mate. Touch the girl or Nathan, an' Ah'll kick yer fuckin' head in. Yer no' on the subs the night. The clown that took yer daughter tae the dance got drunk and broke his leg. He's in the hospital. Mebbe ye should have a word wi' him."

Leo waited. "Well, come on. If it's trouble yer after, I'm here."

Leo was careless with his talent. An alto player, he needed good hands with flexible, supple fingers, firm lips and strong teeth as much as Nathan did.

"I know you two," Horse Jones, said. "You work in the yard, on the submarine. I won't forget this."

"You don't know us, Mister and where we work is none o' yer fuckin' business." Leo stuck his forefinger an inch from the Horse's face. "Touch that wee lassie o' yours an' Ah'll come after ye."

Leo turned to Nathan. "Come on, let's get tae fuck away from this cunt."

Leo drove the car. He was white with barely controlled fury.

"Thanks for stoppin' him, Leo."

"No trouble, Nathan. Ah can't get over the way that big fucker wis gonny hit Dorothy. Imagine; hittin' yer flesh and blood. She's such a nice lassie. I'd kill masel' before ah laid a finger on ma children."

Leo had three beautiful daughters all under five and he loved them. They were great children and Nathan adored having fun with them. Sometimes he watched them to let Leo and his wife go out of an evening. Then he could listen to Leo's wonderful collection of Jazz records. It was a relief to think about Leo's daughters and the music. Good memories cheered him and Nathan considered the rest of the weekend.

He looked forward to Saturday. With Leo, he had a gig with a big band at a dance hall in Glasgow. The music was dull, but the pay was good for an evening's work. In the early morning he'd practise quietly and then, mid morning, travel to Glasgow to The Athenaeum for a lesson in music theory. In the afternoon, he attended a lesson with his teacher of trumpet, Thomas Youngman, Principal Trumpet with the National Orchestra.

But Nathan was unsettled and jangled with nervous energy. He wanted to talk about Dorothy Jones, to tell someone that he'd just met this lovely girl. He wondered how the hell he could see her again. Right now, it would be so good just to say something nice about her. But he was afraid of being mocked.

"Whit dae ye think, Leo; how old is that girl?"

"Dorothy? Seventeen, mebbe eighteen." He grinned. "Don't tell me ye fancy her. Man, yer twenty five; ye'll get done fur baby snatchin'."

"Just wondering, that's all. She's no' really my type."

It had turned out a fine night; the rain was off and a full moon was on the sky, bathing the streets of the town in soft yellow light. Leo let Nathan out at the Square and he walked back up Ann Street and along Galt Place to enjoy the moon lit views of the town, the shipyards and the river.

It had been a long time since Nathan had warm thoughts of a woman. Several times, girls he'd liked brushed him off when they found out he was illegitimate. But that night, he forgot these bitter disappointments and suppressed doubts that Dorothy was too young. As he fell asleep the images of Dorothy Jones came, and he felt he could touch her. As he drifted over, he gave in to hope that this slender, quiet, lovely girl might like him, quite forgetting that he had no idea how he might see her again.

Sunday night and they were a quintet. Christopher Lejune came and Nathan was glad to see him. It must have been a rush to come up for he was in uniform. He played tenor saxophone and when off duty from the US Air Force Base at Prestwick, liked to sit in with the band. He'd met Leo at a gig down in Ayrshire. Chris was a good friend.

"Nathan," Chris said. "How you doin'?"

"Good, Chris; you?"

Chris slung the instrument, holding it in with his left hand. He nodded and raised his right thumb.

"C Jam Blues?"

C Jam Blues; a good number to open and Chris counted out the beat: "A one, two, a one two three four." It would get the attention of the small audience and a few couples, keen on dancing might take the floor. If they could dance to what they played the quintet didn't mind, but on Sunday evenings they played for themselves.

Four numbers played that first hour, and Chris, who loved the Blue Note sound moved them from C Jam Blues to Art Blakey's Moanin' and further out. He was an inspiration; they all played better when Chris was there. The last number, their swinging version of Three Coins In a Fountain, Nathan had his jacket off, tie loosened.

Nathan mopped his brow, tightened the tie, put on his jacket; and then he saw Dorothy Jones standing near the door. There was a girl with her and she definitely wanted to be somewhere else.

"Chris, those two girls by the door; chat up the mousey one for me."

"I like the other one," Chris teased.

"Come on, Chris," Nathan said.

"OK, OK, I'll do it."

"Hello, Dorothy," Nathan said, holding her hand for a moment.

"Hello, Nathan. That was wonderful. I've never heard anything like it."

"Good."

Nathan felt warm and glad that she'd come, but tried to bottle down his euphoria, fearing that he might get it wrong and say something too familiar; too intimate and unsuitable. That would ruin everything. He felt very tender towards her and guessed that she'd taken risks to come to the Club. He felt guilty about his erection and would die if she noticed. But the lighting in the Club was dim, and he felt safe from embarrassment.

Nathan's mouth was dry from excitement. Finally, he found his voice. "What's your friend's name?"

"Audrey. She's my cousin and I'm staying with her tonight. She's a little uncomfortable."

Chris was charming Audrey, smiling warmly, pointing to the instruments, miming playing his tenor. She'd pressed herself against the wall of the room, her face split by a mouthfull of white teeth.

"Who's that speaking to her?" Dorothy said.

"The black man? That's Christopher Lejune. Chris. He's a good friend of ours."

"He's very handsome in his uniform."

Chris always managed to look hip; the working girl's Sidney Poitier. In spite of an hour's energetic playing, he remained cool and sweat free.

"I'm going outside for ten minutes," Nathan said. "You want to come?"

"Thank you."

Dorothy had on her good Sunday clothes for visiting her cousin, a neat costume, navy jacket and straight skirt. She wore dressy, but sensible shoes. It made her look rather prim for a girl of seventeen but did not hide her prettiness. She stood out from the club crowd.

"Take your coat, it might be chilly." If she left it in the room, it might get stolen by one of the riff-raff.

It was a fine night and still light as he steered Dorothy across the road to the food stall that opened on weekends. It wasn't much but it was clean; the man and wife who ran it liked the band.

"The coffee is milky and sweet," Nathan said. "The tea is strong and sweet, and they do hot rolls. Try one on sliced sausage?"

"All right. Thank you."

Nathan turned to look at her and in the strong lights of the stall, saw that she had on make up, a layer of foundation cream and a pale lip stick. He liked her better without it. She looked up smiling and he saw the shadow of a bruise on her right cheek. Without thinking, he reached out and instinctively Dorothy drew back from his hand.

"What happened to your face?"

She looked away, but he knew that Horse Jones had struck Dorothy. "Nothing happened. I don't want to talk about it." Nathan let the tips of his fingers touch the bruise and she didn't flinch.

The food came and they bit into the hot roll and sausage. Dorothy sipped the hot, sweet tea. "It's good."

Back inside, Chris reading Nathan's mind suggested a change of mood. "Let's do ballads. Melancholy Baby, OK?"

Chris played nuanced variations of the melody linking with Chuck's delicate bass line. Joe upped the tempo, a swinging four-four, the cymbals and hi-hat, lifting the song. Leo and Nathan played fast, improvising to the edge of the melody. The dancers stopped.

He was glad she liked his music. Nathan knew they'd played well and in Melancholy Baby he'd been close to saying what he felt about seeing Dorothy again. But it wasn't enough. He had to say more.

They'd been rehearsing a new number that needed more work. But he knew that the song had what he wanted to say. "The new one?" Nathan said.

He coughed into the mike and the room went quiet. "We want to do a song for a friend of ours," Nathan said, waving to Dorothy. She smiled.

Nathan liked to sing and concentrated on the mood of the song. The understanding in the band was deep and intuitive. They wanted to lift Nathan higher.

"Have you met Miss Jones?
Someone said as we shook hands, She was just Miss Jones to me.
And then I said, Miss Jones, you're a girl who understands
I'm a man who must be free.
And all at once I lost my breath, and all at once was scared to death,
And all at once I owned the earth and sky.
And now I've met Miss Jones, and we'll keep on meeting till we die,
Miss Jones and I."

Nathan put the mute in the Bach and he and Leo played it taut and emotional. He sang perfectly for the song belonged to Dorothy Jones.

"And all at once I lost my breath, and all at once was scared to death,
And all at once I owned the earth and the sky.
Now I've met Miss Jones, and we'll keep on meeting till we die,
Miss Jones and I, Miss Jones and I, Miss Jones and I."

A last chorus, reprising the melody. Nathan heard Chuck bowing deep, romantic chords. Joe working with mallets, muffled beats on drums and soft ringing of cymbals brought the song to an end.

"So how was it?" Nathan said.

Audrey smirked. Dorothy smiled. "I like your singing and it's a nice song. I'm embarrassed, but thank you."

"How are you getting home?"

"We'll walk. It's not so far and it isn't very late."

Audrey headed for the lavatory. Visiting that squalid room would shock her.

Nathan held Dorothy's coat. "Can I call you? Its probably better if I call you. What's your surname?"

"Forrest, Nathan Forrest."

IIe gave her his number "Good night, Dorothy. I'm glad you came."

"I will call, Nathan."

She did call several times the following week, but Nathan told Ma to say he was out. Sunday night's happiness vanished and by mid week he'd wrapped himself in despair: worrying that he was too old; that she was too young. He hid behind Horse Jones' drunken temper, an excuse for not returning her calls.

But he was afraid that it would end badly when she discovered he was illegitimate. He wrote her off; just a kid that didn't matter. He was sorry when she stopped calling.

Nathan tried to move on. There was overtime at the yard. The next Sunday was the last session at the club before they stopped for the summer. Midweek, the band was rehearsing for a couple of good gigs Leo had arranged down the coast and Nathan worked on the new arrangements. He almost forgot about Dorothy Jones.

"Nathan, when are you goin' to stop wi' that piano and trumpet? Yer breakfast's nearly ready," Ma yelled from the kitchen.

"Ten minutes, Ma. Ah'm about finished."

It was a beautiful June morning close to Noon. The sun shone in the open window and he saw the old bat that lived in the tenement flats across the common drying green, arms folded, scowling. He picked up the Bach and removed the mute, walking to the window, blasting out the opening notes of You Made Me Love You, finishing with ragged bugle calls. She slammed her window shut and disappeared into the room.

Nathan finished the eggs, bacon and toast before Ma was half way through hers. "You'll have ulcers at the rate ye eat, Nathan."

He grunted as he spread marmalade on a last slice of toast and re-filled his cup from the teapot hidden by its green cosy.

"It's a grand day, Nathan Forrest, and Ah' hope you're no' gonny spend it tootlin' on that trumpet. It's time ye went oot and got some fresh air."

"Somethin' wrong, Ma; are ye no' well?"

"Ach away wi' ye, Nathan. I'm fine and well ye know it. Get some fresh air in yer lungs, that'll be good for ye."

There was a tentative knock at the front door. Ma, finished with her breakfast, closed her knife and fork. "Ah'll get it."

He heard a young, tentative voice: a girl's voice. "Is Nathan here; could I speak to him?"

"Come away in, lassie."

"Hello, Nathan," Dorothy Jones said as she came into the kitchen.

He stood, awkward, worried about his old, scuffed slippers, the faded jeans and the white T Shirt. But a jetstream of happiness shot through Nathan. Then he blushed, ashamed for refusing Dorothy's calls. Dorothy pretended not to notice.

Ma stared at him. "Huv ye been taken poorly, Nathan? Ye've turned a queer colour."

"No, no. Hello, Dorothy. How are you?"

"I'm well, Nathan, but I worried about you when you didn't answer my calls."

"Ah, you're the lassie that phoned, then," Ma said.

"Yes, I am."

Dorothy wore a red summer dress of soft cotton with a small, white fleur de lis motif. It had a high collar, three quarter sleeves and a full skirt. Her pale, white stockings and smart sandals were so girlish. She carried a white sun hat and saw him looking at it. She shrugged and smiled, "I needed it for church and anyway, I burn."

He felt tender and warm standing beside her and he wanted to hold her and say how sorry he was.

"Is there somethin' wrong wi' you, Nathan Forrest?" Ma said. "Where's yer manners?"

"Sorry. Ma, this is a new friend of mine, Dorothy Jones. Dorothy, this is Ma."

Ma and Dorothy smiled as they shook hands. Dorothy said "How do you do?" "Pleased to meet you," Ma said.

Ma got Dorothy seated at table and put a cup of tea and two slices of lightly fried dumpling in front of her.

"I've had breakfast, Ma."

"Go on, yer just a wee slip of a thing. It's good."

Dorothy drank deeply from her teacup and soon the dumpling was gone. She ate with relish and Nathan loved it; just like the evening at the club when he took her to the food stall and they drank tea and ate hot rolls with sliced sausage. "Would you like to go for a walk?" Nathan said.

"Yes, I'd like that."

"When will ye be back, Nathan?" Ma asked.

He looked at Dorothy. "What are you doing at six?"

"Going home. My mother left something prepared. She and my father are away visiting for the day."

"Come back here, then," Ma said. "It's miserable eating yersel'."

"Thank you. That's very kind."

Nathan freshened up, choosing his best navy slacks and the new blue shirt that had been washed and ironed to perfection by Ma. He folded the cuffs back and thought about polishing his already well-polished old, comfortable loafers. Then worried that he'd stain the shirt with black shoe polish and decided there was just enough time to give the loafers a good dusting. He wanted to make this a happy afternoon.

Back in the kitchen, Ma looked him over. "Well, Ah'm gled to see yer dressed fit for Sunday at long last."

Dorothy smiled approvingly and made eyes at him. She excused herself for a few minutes.

"That's a nice young girl, Nathan."

"Ah know."

Dorothy came back to the kitchen. "Are we ready?"

Nathan took her east, figuring that as she lived in the west, it would be new to her. They crossed Provident Street, entering the park, and stood at the War Memorial. They walked round admiring the grey granite sparkling in the June sun, the bronze angel mounting the prow of an ancient ship fronting the monument and the bronze chains anchoring the war memorial to granite columns at each corner.

The frieze of Gothic letters on the four sides of the base recorded the fields of sacrifice: Palestine, Mesopotamia, Italy, Flanders, Gallipoli, France; and the Naval engagements at the Falklands, Jutland and Zebrugge. Further down the base of the memorial was another frieze: men crouching alongside lions; man and beast joined in suffering.

"The men from Westburn," Dorothy said. "They fought everywhere."

"Yes, they did," Nathan, said. "My grandfather used to take me to the Armistice Day parade," Nathan said. "He was in Flanders."

"I see," Dorothy said.

1958 and the Great War was etched in living memory. Beneath the stoic faces of Westburn, pain lurked and time had not healed the wounds of lost sons, dead lovers, and husbands.

"They call it the Well Park," Nathan said moving away from the war memorial. "After my Grandfather died, I used to come here and sit. It's peaceful on sunny days."

They walked through the park, under the oaks and plane trees, past smooth lawns dappled by sunlight. They came to the Old Well dating from 1629, sealed. They admired the sandstone canopy crowning the well, resting on four short Corinthian columns that had been executed by the hand of an artisan.

"Oh I like it," Dorothy said. "Just look at the doves carved on the corners. Why, they're softened and rounded with age and weather. It's simple and beautiful."

Children were busy on the swings and the chute, their cries of pleasure muted by the warm sun. Old men in Sunday best sat on benches warming their bones, glancing at their newspapers.

"It's lovely here," Dorothy said. "It's the first time I've been to the park."

They looked across the river and to the mountains that Nathan loved when the shabbiness of Westburn got him down. "First time?"

"Yes. I was born here but I lived in Hong Kong for years. When my father returned to the shipyard, I was sent to board at a posh school. I've just finished."

"You're looking for a job?"

"Oh gosh, no." She laughed her lovely, girlish laugh. "I'm going to University in October. St Andrew's, to read History and English. I'll be eighteen then." She hesitated. "You see, I did quite well at school and I know I'm lanky, but I was good at games too."

"You're not lanky."

She smiled, squinting into the sun brushing her hat against her leg. He wondered what the hell she saw in him: Nathan Forrest, a welder and part-time musician, trying to play Jazz in this backwater. He figured she should know something more about him.

"I'm twenty-five and I've worked in the yard since I was fourteen," he said.

"All that time?"

"Well, I was in the Army. I went when I was eighteen. Conscription. I was called up."

"What was it like?"

"Terrible. One thing I learnt about the Army is that I never want to be in it, ever again."

They sat on an empty bench, the sun on their backs, the river and mountains to the front.

"Tell me about the Army."

So he told her that he'd served in a Highland Regiment, the infantry. At first he was stationed in dreary Fort George up north. When they discovered he welded, he was on loan to the motor pool doing repairs. Later, Nathan sat in with some of the players in the Regimental band. A cornet player was ill and he performed a stint in the band.

"Did you wear a kilt?

"Yes."

"Oh, Nathan. You in a kilt," she said, smothering laughter with her hand.

"That's how I felt about it. The hard bit was when the Battalion was sent to Korea and I reverted to rifleman."

"Was that bad?"

Nathan was silent as he remembered one attack by waves of Chinese that almost over ran the position. They were beaten back with great difficulty. He shrugged non-committally.

"It was dirty: hot in the summer and cold in the winter. I never got used to the way the Chinese sounded attacks on bugles. I was glad to get home. They let me do a bit more welding in the motor pool, and I hung around the band before I was demobbed."

"I see."

Nathan learnt more about welding and was better at it when he got out of the Army. The personal breakthrough was the final stint in the Regimental band playing the cornet. His technique improved and finally, he got a firm hand on reading music.

"They tried to get me to sign on again. Promised me a permanent place in the band."

They moved to the edge of the park and looked down at a derelict house dominating the northwest approach, its windows boarded, the stonework sooty and damp.

"That house must have been beautiful. Look at the chimneys: they're so slender and elegant."

Dorothy was right but Nathan lived so close to it that he often walked by without seeing.

"Yes. It was built in the 17th Century, the Baron Baillie's House."

"Why doesn't the town restore it?"

"Anything old here, the politicians want to knock it down, not fix it up. They call it progress."

Nathan pictured the new, already shabby estates ringing Westburn. He preferred the fading elegance of Galt Place to the drab uniformity of the politicians' concrete shoeboxes.

"Have a look sometime at the housing estates they've built. You'll see what they mean by progress."

The clock in the tower of the Clyde Kirk chimed quarter past two and they looked across to it.

"What an elegant steeple. You're so lucky to live near it, Nathan."

"The clock sometimes wakens me at night."

For Nathan it was just another church with a steeple, a Protestant Church of less interest than the Catholic Church he'd rejected. But, when Dorothy mentioned it he looked at the building anew. It was a beautiful church; so much more than a temple of bourgeois spirituality marooned in his part of Westburn.

Nathan took pride in the the close feeling he had for Westburn. He showed Dorothy the Dutch Gabled House built in 1755, elegant still, in its cloak of shabby disrepair.

"What a shame. It's so sad and neglected. It needs a lover to take care of it."

"Lover to take care of it."

The shock of Dorothy's words left him feeling warm. But, he felt the stab of pain, remembering the wreckage of a youthful crush. When he was sixteen, Nathan met a girl at a dance and had gone out with her several times. He'd walked home with the girl, a freckled little pudding. At the entrance to her tenement, she turned on him.

"Ma mother says your nuthin' but a bastard an Ah've no' tae see ye again."

Surely it would be different with Dorothy?

They admired the Lyle Fountain at the centre of the square, built in eighteen seventy nine. The fountain covered by a wrought iron dome had around its edges the shields commemorating the local gentry: Dunlops, Baines, Farrens, Wallace of Kelly, Scott and Morton, Crawfurd of Cartsburn. These families believed in 'God Speed Westburn,' but it would need a great impetus from their heirs and successors to shift the town out of its present lassitude.

"Sure, they made Westburn," Nathan said, "But it was people like me that built the place and the ships and engines. You'd think the names of a few workmen might've appeared on the fountain."

They turned from the fountain, and saw the ragged edges of the gable ends on the Municipal Buildings, proud old lime and mortar pointing sticking out between the bricks. Cowan's Corner demolished in the Blitz and not yet fully repaired.

Heading east, they passed the Long Well dug in 1682 at the bottom of Duff Street; it had never been grand: by 1958 it was a melancholy place; a gloomy canyon of shabby tenements.

They walked on, passing several bombsites. Once, tenements stood there until flattened by German bombers in 1941. The patterned tiles covering the floor of tenement entrances remained visible through the tramped earth and weeds. Westburn had not yet fully recovered from the effects of the war.

Nathan stopped and looked around up to the park and back to the square, and swept the view with his hand. "I explored every nook and crannie here when I was a boy. It's my place."

Later, they strolled on the Old Quay licking ice cream cones. "Mmm," she said, her pink tongue darting out for another taste. Dorothy pointed her cone at the Georgian Customs House. "The honey coloured stone, it's beautiful."

"Giffnock sand stone," Nathan said. "The emigrants to North America and the West Indies used to leave from here."

"In those awful wooden ships?"

"They must have. They say Captain Kidd was born in Westburn."

"The pirate? Golly."

Gosh and golly, schoolgirl slang. So there were people who spoke that way. But he liked it when she said it; he really liked this girl.

"Wait a minute" Dorothy said. "I remember something about the Customs House. My English teacher mentioned it. John Galt, the novelist worked there, a clerk."

"Never heard of him."

"Oh, he's quite famous. He wrote Annals of the Parish. I didn't like it. He travelled with Byron in the Mediterranean. Something about arranging trade agreements. Your address, Galt Place has to be named for him."

"Is that right enough?"

They moved closer to the building and read the commemorative plaque. The builders, former soldiers, fought in the Napoleonic Wars. They started work in eighteen sixteen and finished three years later.

"There's so much history here, Nathan. Thank you for bringing me."

They moved to the end of the Quay near the crumbling boom defence depot to be far away from other people. They sat on a bollard, its dark blue steel warm by the sun.

"How are things at home?" Nathan said.

She looked at her sandals and the brim of her sun hat hid her profile. "My dad's a troubled man. I worry about him."

Nathan felt they had to share secrets; take risks, hiding nothing that could surface painfully later.

"My father probably should have the top job at the yard in Hong Kong, but he didn't get it. Afterwards, our life changed completely. He drank far too much and the company sent him to dry out."

"Did it work?"

"For a while and then the drinking started again and they sent him home."

Dorothy shuddered, "He hit my mother and when I tried to stop him, he hit me."

Nathan touched her hand resting on the bollard. "I'm so sorry."

"Well, it's come to a head. Today, he and my mother are at lunch with the Managing Director. The company want him to supervise work on two destroyers for the Turkish Navy. It's an important job. My father is a gifted Naval Architect. He'll be in Istanbul for three or four months. I'm afraid if he doesn't control his drinking, the company will sack him. My mother's going with him; trying to keep him right. I wish there was something more I could do."

"I think it's up to him, now."

"Do you drink, Nathan?"

"No, I don't. I find everything in the music. I play better without it."

"I thought all the men here drank."

"I drank a bit when I got out of the Army. I went out with an older woman for a while. She was a singer I worked with. The drink and her didn't agree with me. I haven't seen her in a long time."

"I see," Dorothy said and pressed his hand.

Nathan looked up and saw a black suited man walking briskly towards them. The priest doffed the heavy, dark felt hat and looked as if he would stop and speak. Nathan gave him a curt nod and turned away. The priest replaced his hat and hurried on.

"Who was that man?"

"A priest from my school days, Brendan Toner. We never got on."

Dorothy, worried that Nathan might turn gloomy, pointed to the river. "Oh, look at that old ship."

She was an old duchess of the sea with her woodbine funnel and counter stern. They listened to the rhythmic thump of the ship's reciprocating steam engine coming over the water.

"The Santander; a Spanish ship," Nathan said. "The yard built her in eighteen ninety-seven. I worked on her last week."

"Gosh," Dorothy said. She watched the Santander heading down river to the open sea. Dorothy was lovely and Nathan wanted to hold her. "The Santander's gone now," Dorothy said.

"She's a graceful old lady," Nathan said.

"I like Ma," Dorothy said.

"I meant the Santander," Nathan said.

"Oops. Sorry."

"Just kidding. I like Ma too. She brought me up."

"What's Ma's name; and your grandfather?"

"Millicent. Her friends call her Millie, but she likes Ma too. My grandfather's name was James."

"What happened to your Mum and Dad?"

"My Mum died when I was born. Her name was Olive. She was good looking. My father was a seaman, name of William Calderwood. He died in an accident before I was born so he's always been remote. That's all I know about him. I've never used Calderwood."

"You don't know anything about him?"

"No. Ma said he was an orphan and a neighbour's son brought him home on leave and he met my mum. Ma was heartbroken when my mum died. She was eighteen, an only child."

"How awful. I'm sorry."

"Look, Dorothy, I'm illegitimate. It's bad enough yet but it was grim in nineteen thirty-three when I was born. I'm twenty-five but to some people I'm just a bastard."

"Well, I'm not one of them, Nathan."

"A priest tried to take me away from Ma and my Grandfather," Nathan said.

"What happened?"

"The Parish Priest, an Irishman, came to the house. He told Ma and James to deliver me from bastardy and give me to a respectable and loving Catholic family."

"How dreadful."

"My Grandfather told him to get out of the house. Ma and James adopted me. It's hard not knowing your mother; there's no happy ending."

"Have people been unkind to you?"

"In school they called me a bastard, and I fought them. In the Army I quarreled with a soldier who called me a bastard. Once I stumbled at drill and a Corporal called me a stupid bastard. I challenged him, and got a thick ear and seven days KP. Out of the Army, I quit fighting over it; fights made no difference. But here, people I liked avoided me and a couple of girls stood me up. It doesn't matter to my friends now."

"That's dreadful."

Nathan felt that he might as well give her the rest of the bad news. "You know I'm a Catholic, don't you? I gave it up years ago. Toner, that priest who passed us; well, he said I was born out of wedlock."

"That's so cruel, Nathan. I assumed you were a Catholic."

"And you're not bothered about it?"

"Of course not."

Nathan felt that he could tell this girl anything about himself. He told her about the hatred between Catholics and Protestants down the yard: engineers tended to be Protestants and the Catholics welders, burners, caulkers, riveters and platers. "We're called the Black Squad."

"I see," Dorothy said.

"Protestants have called me a Tim, a Teague, a Pape, a Fienian and worse. There's no escape, Dorothy: once a Tim, always a Tim. The Catholics are just as bad. I want nothing to do with any of it."

He told Dorothy about the snowy day when he and a few others walked home from school through a tough Protestant neighbourhood. A gang of boys threw hard snowballs with stones in the middle.

"I was thirteen. I got hit on the head and knocked out. In the Infirmary they put a couple of stitches in the wound."

But Nathan didn't tell Dorothy that the Protestant gang leader, shouted "Fuck The Pope." A week later he and two others ambushed that older boy and gave him a kicking.

"I never heard of any trouble mentioned at school in Hong Kong; and it was never spoken of in my school in Edinburgh. Nathan, I like you just as you are."

"Kids stuff, load a shite," Nathan had said one day down the yard, to an unfortunate apprentice he'd seen holding hands with his girlfriend. "Yer fuckin' head's wasted." This was Nathan's public, hard man mask.

Nathan's warm manner said that he liked Dorothy and she guessed that he needed a sign from her. She folded her hand into Nathan's as they walked back to Galt Place, and Nathan clasped her hand.

They turned for a last look before they left the Old Quay. Eastwards lay the panorama of the cranes, the stocks, fitting out berths and the entrance to the Graving Dock: places that pumped the lifeblood through Westburn.

"A good day then, Dorothy?"

"Oh, gosh, yes But it's not over, is it? I mean we are going back to Ma's, aren't we?"

"Of course we are. Did you think I'd let you get away?"

Dorothy's gesture, the presence of her hand in his hand, made Nathan confident, and he stopped her, covering her hand with both of his hands. "I'm really sorry I didn't answer your calls. I didn't want to cause trouble. I'm so glad you came today. I've thought a lot about you since that night we first met."

"I thought a lot about you too," Dorothy said. "I wanted to see you again."

Dorothy looked at her plate. "What is it?"

"It's herrings dressed in oatmeal," Ma said, "with new potatoes and chopped cabbage, and after that we'll have fruit compote."

"I've never tasted herrings in oatmeal."

"Never?" Nathan said.

"Well, I grew up in Hong Kong."

Ma had prepared a light dinner for such a hot June evening. She filled the glasses with cold water from the jug on the table, and Dorothy took a sip. She cut into the fish and tentatively chewed on a forkful. Ma and Nathan waited.

Nathan and Ma liked visitors. Ma threw a party two or three times a year for the band. Leo and his family were frequent visitors. She had a soft spot for Chris, a serviceman far from home and she and Nathan looked forward to the special days when their friend, Ma's old employer, Mr. Montague Solomon came to Galt Place. Monty Solomon; Mr. Monty to Nathan: his mentor and father figure whom he often went to for advice. But this was the first time a girl, a friend of Nathan's, dined with them.

Ma, confident about her cooking, was unfazed entertaining a girl from the middle-class, especially as she liked Dorothy Jones on sight and sensed that Dorothy returned the liking. But Nathan worried that Dorothy would look down on them.

Dorothy cut the herring into small pieces and chewed delicately. She had beautiful manners. "Mmm," Dorothy murmured and then swallowed. "Oh, it's very good."

"An' it's good for ye, oily fish," Ma said. "Improves yer brains."

"Dorothy has plenty of brains," Nathan said. "She's going to St Andrew's University."

"Ah'll tidy up," Ma said. "Show Dorothy yer records, Nathan. He must have every Jazz record. An' he plays the piano as well."

"I'd like that, but I'd better think about going. My parents will be home soon. If I'm not in, they'll wonder where I am."

"I'll walk with you," Nathan said.

"Ye can hear them next time ye come," Ma said.

Nathan caught the question in Dorothy's eye. Would she be visiting again? He walked with her most of the way home. He didn't want her parents to see them together. It was a fine clear night. She'd folded her hand into his as soon as they left Galt Place.

"That was a lovely day, Nathan, and I so enjoyed my dinner."

He clasped her hand more firmly. She smiled.

"Will I see you again?" Nathan said.

"Oh yes. I'd like that; and you'll play the piano for me?"

Chapter Two

The old MFV ferry took them across the river, cruising through the gentle swell of the ebbing tide and they surrendered to the rhythmic pulse of the diesel engine. They were happy sitting for'ard on deck, the sun and the breeze in their faces, Dorothy, resting her head on Nathan's shoulder for much of the crossing.

It was five weeks since they met: the best time in their lives. Nathan had never known such openness and affection as came from Dorothy. He was falling in love with her.

He'd never said that he loved any woman and lacked the confidence to tell Dorothy that he loved her though he wanted to, and tortured himself about when he might tell her.

Songs often brought thoughts of Dorothy. When he listened to Billie Holiday sing Body and Soul he thought he could tell her that was how he felt, but he didn't. Nathan knew Dorothy had affection for him, but dreaded that she'd tell him they were just good friends. He couldn't go on with her if that happened, so he hung on, skirting around his growing love for her, dreaming that Dorothy might say she loved him. He was glad that Dorothy idealized his welding skills and the romance of being a Jazz musician.

They disembarked, walking from the pier to the beach, hands touching. Nathan suggested a place among low rocks surrounded by clean sand for their picnic. The spot had good views across the river to Westburn.

They walked to the edge of the water and shaded their eyes. Westwards lay Dunoon and the Argyll hills; to the south, opposite, three miles across the river the Esplanade lined by grand Victorian villas.

"Westburn," Nathan said. "It looks all right from here, doesn't it?"

"Yes, it does look rather nice," Dorothy said. "Distance makes the heart grow fonder."

Nathan expertly skimmed flat stones across the smooth surface of the water unable to resist showing off a little.

"It's a beautiful trumpet you have," Dorothy said. "When did you get it?"

"Its American. A Bach Mercury, a present from Mr. Monty when I got out of the Army. Bach instruments and mouthpieces; they're so well designed and the quality is wonderful. I look after it."

"When did you become a Jazz musician?"

"I started young."

When he was ten, Nathan began playing the cornet in St Michael's Silver Band sponsored by his parish church. He stayed with the band until he left school and gave up the Faith.

"It was Monty Solomon, Mr. Monty, got me interested in Jazz. He's a great friend. Ma used to work for him."

Mr. Monty heard from Ma about Nathan's love of the cornet and lent him records. At fourteen life was never the same after Nathan worked his way through the recordings of Louis Armstrong's Hot Five and Hot Seven. He and Mr. Monty enjoyed a good-natured dispute about the greatest Armstrong record. For Mr. Monty, it was Potato Head Blues; Nathan said it was Muskrat Ramble.

Mr. Monty loaned Nathan the money to buy his first instrument, an old silver Conn trumpet. He made Nathan a present of a new mouthpiece. Nathan acquired enough playing technique and reading music in the silver band to make progress on his own.

"Monty Solomon, Mr. Monty," Dorothy said. "They're funny names for a Scot."

"He's Jewish from Odessa. His family came here when he was a child." Nathan said. "He's been very good to us and Ma is fond of him. I've got a lot of time for Mr. Monty."

"Can I meet him?"

"Sure. He'll be coming soon. We have a meal, sometimes a wee party. Ma makes special food for him. He likes to hear the band playing. It'd be nice if you're there."

"The band is wonderful," Dorothy said. "You never play a song the same way, and the music swings. It's exciting and puzzling. Chris is such a good player, but you're right up there beside him."

Nathan grinned, flushing, embarrassed but pleased too. "If we're getting it right, every time we play a song it'll be different."

"You always get it right."

"We've been playing together for two years, and I don't know how long it can last. It's very intense, and Jazz wise, we couldn't be closer. I mean Leo isn't Art Pepper and Chris isn't Coltrane, and I'm not Freddie Hubbard. But we're playing good things; the music, it just hangs together. We understand one another, and there's trust. Right now, we really know what we're doing; and we're doing it well for its own sake."

"It's just wonderful."

"It's a long way from the rough gigs in the clubs and lodges when I started. I put in the hours with the band, Dorothy. I know the Bach; it's a part of me. I know where it can take me, and I reach for that."

Dorothy drew him out, creating her personal mosaic of Nathan Forrest, Jazz musician. He'd caught her up in the music. One day soon, he'd tell Dorothy that he loved her.

"You're a Romantic, Nathan."

"A Romantic? Never heard of it."

"They were artists and intellectuals; eighteenth century people. I studied them in school. They adored emotions and imagination and hated rules. Rebels, I suppose."

"Me an artist; a rebel? You must be kidding. Anyway, I don't hate rules, not the rules of music. I go to work, I mind my business, and everything else is Jazz."

"Oh, I don't know. You care so much about Jazz. I thought you might be a Romantic. Someday you might want another kind of life. More music and less shipyard, if you see what I mean."

"Well, I guess I should think about it." He didn't want to think about it. Despite its rough edges and the creeping decay, Nathan was comfortable in Westburn. He loved Ma and had a duty towards her. Nathan knew musicians reduced by the grind of a job down the yard and the artistic poverty of Westburn, but refused to change his life.

"Did you really mean it when you said that outside work, everything else is Jazz?" Dorothy said.

He let his guard down and surprised Dorothy by taking both her hands and kissing her. "The music; it's important. You know that; but it's just one thing. Days I don't see you, well, they're empty."

"I know."

They laid out the picnic. Nathan was surprised by what Dorothy had prepared: a wicker basket containing one thermos of coffee, another with cold, homemade lemonade, portions of cold, roast chicken and salad, crusty bread, already buttered, and melamine cups, plates and cutlery. There were dainty, blue chequered cotton napkins, a blanket to sit on.

"Did you do all this?"

"Yes, of course. I learned to cook in school."

Nathan's idea of a picnic was to wrap a couple of Ma's thick cut sandwiches in grease proof paper, fill a thermos with strong, sweet tea and pack it in his old Army knapsack.

They enjoyed the food and the river views. "I went to the library and looked up your name," Dorothy said. "I wanted to find out what it means."

"Tell me."

"It means a Gift from God. It's from the Hebrew."

"What about your name?"

"Well, it's funny, but I looked that up too and Dorothy means a Gift of God. It's from the Greek. Our names mean the same thing."

"The same thing. I like that."

"You're not a bad present, not really; and I like it too, Nathan."

They sat quietly until the position of the sun told them the afternoon was ending.

"Time for the six o'clock ferry," Nathan said, as he packed the picnic basket and put the blanket in his knapsack and they walked back to the pier.

With Dorothy's parents away in Istanbul, their attraction grew exponentially. For those few months, Dorothy was staying with her Aunt Zoë, her father's younger sister. She knew that Dorothy was seeing Nathan and wanted to meet him.

"You're invited to tea at Aunt Zoë's on Sunday," Dorothy said as they settled down on the ferry for the sail back to Westburn.

This would be the first time he'd meet anyone called Zoë. "Why? Does she want to see whether I'm suitable?"

"Please, Nathan. She's a nice person, a free spirit. She teaches History at the Academy Grammar. It's a small, private school for girls; quite posh; and she's a passionate Socialist."

"OK. I'll be on my best behaviour."

"Nathan, just be yourself."

Nathan suspected that Aunt Zoë would be an aging version of the Rugby Club women: braying voice, drooping arse and sagging tits; and determined to assess his worth.

Nathan crossed the threshold of Zoë's house, tripped on the doormat, and stumbled into the hall. "Sorry," he said.

Dorothy laughed, but it did not shift the frosty look on Zoë's face. "Hello, Nathan. I've heard a lot about you," Zoë said, from thinly parted lips, assessing him from hooded eyes.

"Pleased to meet you, Miss," Nathan said, uncomfortable out of his milieu,

Zoë was about thirty-five, had Dorothy's build and was dark. But, there was a look of Dorothy's father that made Nathan uneasy. He liked her stylish, gamine Audrey Hepburn haircut; dressed like her too: white blouse with high collar, full, dark navy skirt, navy shoes with low heels. Zoë had shapely legs with fine ankles.

Zoë saw that Nathan was working class; probably a Catholic. His grey suit was of good wool and well made, but of vulgar cut. The button down collar of his white shirt was simply ridiculous, and the wine coloured wool tie, nondescript. Grudgingly, she approved of his polished shoes and she had to admit that in a coarse way, he wasn't bad looking. Spitefully, Zoë concluded that his appearance was a crude attempt to look like one of those American Jazz musicians who appeared in the French films she watched.

Zoë was angry that Dorothy found this creature attractive. Why could she not have brought home a nice boy from the Rugby Club, or the Cricket Club? Someone dressed in tasteful, tweed hacking jacket and twill trousers; a nicely checked Vyella shirt complimenting the Club tie; and suede shoes: so middle-class and attractive on a man.

Zoë gave Nathan the imperious look that she used to reduce stubborn pupils. "Nathan, Miss will never do, I'm not quite the Maiden Lady yet. You must call me Zoë."

Nathan saw Zoë's look and heard the scorn. His school days were long over, and he resolved to give no ground to her.

"Dorothy," Zoë said. "Please be a dear and see that everything's all right in the kitchen.

"It is all right. I looked at everything just before Nathan came in."

Dorothy's refusal rattled Zoë. She hated having her strategy for dealing with this fellow deflected.

Dorothy admired her aunt, but had felt the edge of Zoë's sharp tongue, and wanted to stay with Nathan. He felt the quiet stretching to sunset.

Zoë had a duty to perform. "Dorothy told me how good you were at the dance, rescuing her and taking her home. Thank you. I suppose my brother forgot to say so."

"Yes," Nathan said.

"You're so discreet, Nathan. How tactful of you." Zoë said. She waved her hand. "Dorothy said that you're a welder. Are you a good welder?"

"He's a very good welder," Dorothy said. "Nathan works on the submarines for the Royal Navy."

"I've heard that many of the welders are Catholic," Zoë said. "Are Catholics suited to the trade?"

"Never thought about it; maybe it's the Sacraments or the Holy Ghost. He's the Man; that's what makes us good welders. I can weld anything."

"Do you follow Glasgow Celtic, that Catholic football team?"

"I've never been to a Celtic game."

Nathan tried to lighten the mood, anxious that Dorothy would not get caught in the middle of the fight that Zoë seemed intent on having with him. "The welding, well it's OK, it's what

I do for wages. It doesn't compare to playing with the band, but Jazz is a poor living in Westburn."

Zoë held on to an icy silence. She disliked Catholics, looked down on them; and she wasn't interested in Nathan's welding skills, or the band. "So, Nathan, do you read music?"

"Nathan takes a class on music theory at The Athenaeum on a Saturday morning," Dorothy said. "In the afternoon he studies with Thomas Youngman, Principal Trumpet of the SNO."

Zoë gave her niece a dry look and turned to Nathan.

"Of course, I read music," Nathan said. "I'm a musician. I could read from when I was about eleven. The Silver Band insisted everyone learn to read, and the Army was a good training too."

"Nathan was in the Korean War," Dorothy said.

"Really," Zoë said.

"I didn't pick it. The Army sent me."

"Nathan can wear the Butcher's Apron," Dorothy said. "That's what the Jocks called the UN Medal. The ribbon has blue and white stripes."

"Hmm," Zoë said. "So what exactly do you play; is Jazz really music; isn't it simply a lot of noise?"

"You read music, Zoë?"

"I understand the basics."

Nathan jerked his head in the direction of the piano standing on the back wall of the room. "Do you play?"

"I can pass myself."

"So, if I played something right now, you'd know the key, and the time signature; and you'd know when I improvised?"

Zoë flushed, and said nothing. Nathan let her stew. "I'll play and show you. I could teach you."

"Why don't we go in and have tea," Dorothy said. Nathan exchanged a look with Dorothy, keeping his arms resting on his legs, looking straight ahead. He hated veiled rows, but refused to be humbled in front of Dorothy. And he would not allow Dorothy to be humiliated through him.

"Yes, why don't we do that," Zoë said.

"Come Nathan," Dorothy said, leading him to the dining room.

Zoë removed the stopper from the crystal Sherry decanter. "Dorothy, Nathan, care for a glass of Sherry?"

"No thank you," Dorothy said.

"Thanks, but I don't drink," Nathan said.

Zoë poured a good measure into a crystal glass and drank off two thirds of the wine in one swallow. She felt a stab of embarrassment at Nathan's look.

It was the kind of tea Nathan had read about. He let his eyes wander over the table. Dorothy and Zoë had gone to some trouble: a generous plate of tiny, homemade hot sausage rolls resting on doilies, plates of neat sandwiches on brown bread, the crusts trimmed; sardines on toast. He enjoyed the egg and cress sandwiches. The savouries and the excellent tea relieved the earlier tension.

"Thanks, Zoë," Nathan said. "This is wonderful."

Zoë inclined her head, "Dorothy prepared most of it; now and then she let me help."

Dorothy blushed and smiled. Nathan hoped the mood would improve.

"That's nice," Nathan said, nodding to the picture hanging over the fireplace.

"Really," Zoë said, "It's Delacroix's Algerian Women In Their Apartments. What do you like about it?"

"I like the women. They're very attractive. It's relaxed; intimate. The hookah, their bare feet, and slippers lying about. The colours are warm."

"Hmm; and what about the Daumier?"

Nathan looked to his left, to the wall facing the bay windows. He knew nothing of Daumier's The Third Class Carriage. He saw a drab portrait of shabby working people travelling by train. "It's OK."

"Daumier," Zoë said. "He has so much compassion for the poor and the working class. I thought it might appeal to you."

"Ye like that? Ye can huv the real thing any day o' the week. Take a workers' bus, Monday tae Friday. Come doon the yerd. Eat the slop they serve in the canteen an' watch oot fur the pigeons shittin' in yer soup."

He saw the flashes of black rage, her eyes boring into him. "Is that so?" Zoë said.

"Yes, that's so."

Silence. Pancakes and crumpets curled at the edges, rich currant cake grew hard; crumbs fell. The jams and marmalades congealed in their crystal dishes; and the fresh pot of Earl Grey stewed under its tea cosy.

"Nathan," Dorothy said. "I'd like to go for a walk."

"Why; whatever's wrong?" Zoë said.

Nathan rose and pulled Dorothy's chair back from the table, and she moved back. "You know perfectly well what's wrong. You've treated Nathan abominably and I'm ashamed of you."

"Oh, please, Dorothy. No tears. You're being silly."

"You're incredibly rude," Dorothy said. "You must apologize to Nathan.

"In my own house? I'll do no such thing."

They walked in silence for half an hour. Nathan wondered where Dorothy's sweet nature came from. She'd been happy at having him to tea; now she wept salty tears.

"It's a nice sunset over the river," Nathan said. Dorothy nodded, too vexed to speak.

Zoë was some socialist. Nathan imagined her sounding off in front of a class of naive girls. Obviously, she'd never met a bastard and the only contacts she'd had with his people were tradesmen and char ladies. She was a hypocrite.

Nathan saw through Zoë's polite facade to the venomous remarks and contemptuous smile. Down the yard, he'd seen men treated this way, like shit, by arrogant managers. Zoë had intended cutting him to pieces in front of Dorothy. It hadn't worked.

They lingered at the gate. Nathan saw Zoë's silhouette through the curtain and wondered if her hands shook with fury. Zoë watched them from behind a curtain enraged that events had not gone her way.

"I'm sorry that we fell out." Nathan said.

"I'm glad you put Zoë in her place. Nathan, please do something for me."

"Sure; anything."

"Please don't swear again."

"I was sore at Zoë. I wanted to annoy her. But I'm sorry. I promise I won't speak like that again. Will she make trouble with your mother and father?"

"No. That would make her look foolish. Zoë couldn't stand that."

They kissed goodnight. Nathan saw a curtain move. "Will you be all right?"

"I'll be fine. I'll see you on Tuesday evening."

Nathan had expected tolerance from an educated woman, but Zoë's good looks hid a poisoned character. "She's a scrubber," Nathan said.

Nathan left the deserted streets of Valentia behind, recrossing the frontier of Lord Nelson Street back into his side of Westburn. He met few people walking down Walker's Brae. The hum of machinery from the sugar refinery irritated him. Nathan crossed Kip Street listening for the sound of the West Burn flowing beneath the cobbles.

The encounter with Zoë brought worries about an attractive mature woman he'd known. Nathan stopped and listened for the soothing gurgle of running water, but the burn was routed too deep. He walked on and passed the Infirmary on his right and then Shaw Street Infants' School on his left; the jarring memory of Sister Mary Elizabeth, a cruel woman straight from Hell: one of Satan's Concubines. Warm thoughts of the motherly Sister Anna who loved infants

Nathan walked up Ann Street and lingered at the end of Galt Place, resting his arms on the coping stone of the steep retaining wall above the railway. The lights of the house were out, but Ma would lie awake until she heard him come in.

It was a moonless night and a clear sky. He looked at the North Star, and The Plough; Venus was visible. Nathan knew little of stars or planets, but the pale distant light cheered him. He stayed by the wall, gazing over chimneys, and across the river to the darkened hills, and thought about June Connor.

When he met June Connor he was twenty-two, lonely and unsettled two years out of the Army. Nathan was ashamed of his serial screwing and heavy drinking. He'd finished with June almost three years ago. Since he met Dorothy, Nathan regretted the entire episode.

June Connor sang. Her real name was Philomena O'Donnell. She was about thirty-five. One evening Philomena approached as he walked home from the yard. She was small, and the edges of hairpins and rollers made jagged contours on the scarf covering her head; the knot in the scarf jutting above her nose. An untidy smear of bright red lipstick brightened her pasty complexion. The blue work overall hung below her shabby coat and on her feet, scuffed shoes with the stockings rolled down on the tops of woollen ankle socks. Her jaws worked steadily on a wad of chewing gum that she sucked into bubbles; and every few minutes, popped loudly against her front teeth.

"You're Nathan Forrest," she said. "Ye play the trumpet?"

"Ah'm Nathan, an' yes, I play the trumpet."

"Ah'm Philomena O'Donnell, but Ah sing as June Connor." She extended her hand.

Nathan pressed her hand and felt the stump of her second finger; two joints missing. Philomena was an operator in the tin box factory and had caught her hand in a guillotine or double seaming machine.

Philomena liked Jazz and had picked June from June Christie and Connor from Chris Connor. "Bail me oot, will ye? Ah need a trumpet fur a wee gig in a couple of weeks. A Friday night; money's good."

The gig, a Christmas dance for a local engineering firm. It wouldn't stretch Nathan; he'd worked with the bassist and drummer. The dance would end with a selection of standards. "Can ye dae that?"

"Sure. But, Ah want tae rehearse it wi' ye," Nathan said."Ah want to understand how ye work."

"Ach, let's jist busk it."

"Afraid not. We rehearse, or Ah won't take the job."

She grinned lopsidedly, prettily. Some dental butcher had pulled the two teeth behind her right incisor. "Aye, OK. I heard ye were pernickety."

Nathan enjoyed the last part of the gig. The first set was dire, blasting through songs popular with the audience. Philomena sang well, sometimes loudly, but the audience liked a 'belter' who encouraged them to join in: Love Letters In The Sand, Love is a Many Splendoured Thing, Singing The Blues and Volare.

And Philomena was lovely. Bobbed hair framing her face, perfect make up, the little black dress hugging her excellent figure, as she pranced in her heels in front of the band, showing off her shapely legs. Philomena waved the audience on, an out of tune and noisy chorus. The songs bored Nathan, but he played well.

Philomena sang the standards beautifully: Day in Day Out, A Foggy Day, an innocent waif, eyes closed, hands clutching the mike, moving with the quiet rhythm of the bass and drums, swaying provocatively for a swinging Just One Of Those Things. The audience shifted from unruly participation to silent attention.

The last song was Have Yourself a Merry Little Christmas. Philomena was bittersweet for Christmases past as Nathan used the mute, stretching the melody, heightening Philomena's sadness. The band reprised the tune; the tenor worked behind Nathan's horn. Philomena, statuesque, waiting, the points of her breasts moving with her breath. Nathan discarded the mute and Philomena, clutching the mike, eyes closed drawing the song away from Yuletide, slurred words, an invitation to her bed.

"Play wi' me again?" Philomena said.

"Sure," Nathan said. "Ah'd like that."

Walking home that night after the gig, Nathan told her that a better professional name was Philo O'Donnell, but she dismissed it. "People know me as June Connor an' Ah'm stickin' wi' that. But you can call me Philo."

Philomena's voice was good and would have been much better had she studied with a teacher. Nathan mentioned it. "Ye sing well, Philo. Ma teacher could recommend someone. Yer no' too old. Ah'll help reading music."

"Tae Hell wi' it. Ah'm far too busy."

Philomena had reached the apex of her fame, preferring the tawdry glamour of Westburn's shabby clubs and dance halls. Her season in the candlelight brightened by the occasional gig at a golf club or a company dance.

She asked Nathan to come to her flat to look at some new songs. "We can go over them on the piano." After an hour of half hearted practice, she turned to Nathan, "How about it?"

Nathan obliged. One night, he said "Philo, Ah care for you."

"Cut tha' oot," Philomena said. "Jist get up me an' get me aff."

Nathan and Philomena screwed a lot, and she adored sodomy. She persuaded Nathan to try it, "Jist this wan time." A French doctor working at the local infirmary gave her a taste for it when he'd picked her up at a gig.

When Nathan sodomized her it had to be perfect. Philomena's attention to detail was thorough, keeping a tub of Vaseline to lubricate her arse. "Rub it well in. Don't put too much on," she said. "An' put some on yer self."

But Philomena didn't undress. She preferred hiking up her skirt, rolling down her drawers, baring her rear end as she bent across her dressing table to look at her reflection in the mirror. Nathan was surprised by her pink satin corset as he smeared Vaseline on her and himself. He expected something dark, silky, and glamorous. When he got in she lit a cigarette, dragging deeply, grunting until she got off. Often she'd tell Nathan, "That was fuckin' great."

Nathan liked the narcotic of anal screwing. He was curious about Philomena's dedication to sodomy. "Why dae ye like it this way?"

"It's jist so fuckin' good. An' Ah'll no' get a wean. Ah love it. Ah canny get enough o' it."

And they drank. Philomena drank Nathan to a standstill as they went round for round, whisky and beer chasers. They went to a dance in the Dockers' Club where she was singing accompanied by an accordion, fiddle, clarinet, and drums. A couple of dockers insisted on chatting up Philomena, and as the star she revelled in their attentions. Nathan, very drunk objected; he got the hammering of his life while Philomena was singing.

The hiss of steam and moving rolling stock wakened Nathan. He'd no idea why he was lying on the railway. He screamed and staggered clear of the train.

When Nathan hobbled into the streetlights, he saw his own vomit on his torn jacket and pants. Stones cut his left foot where he'd lost a shoe. He touched his swollen left eye and felt round his mouth, relieved that his teeth were intact. The deep ache in his legs and torso got worse, and the dry heaves brought him to his knees.

Ma woke him. "I threw out your suit. It's ruined and that odd shoe as well." She examined the eye and the bruises on her grandson. "Get up. Yer goin' tae the hospital an' Ah'm goin' with ye."

They taped Nathan's ribs and gave him embrocation for his legs. The eye was OK but the swelling needed a dressing. Nathan was off work for a week. That Sunday Ma let him stew. Next morning, he managed to get up for breakfast and she didn't miss him.

"Yer a damned disgrace, Nathan Forrest. Ye'll lose a week's wages bein' off work. Ye could've lost yer eye and that would've ended yer music and yer trade. Don't bother tellin' me whit happened. Ye'll only make me angrier and worry me. Ye can stay here if ye mend yer ways or ye can leave now."

He caught her arm as she turned away. "Ah'm very sorry. It won't happen again. Ah promise."

"See that ye mean it."

"Well, well, if it's no' the World Champion. Nathan, ye need a lesson in boxin'," Philomena said when he appeared at her flat. He told her that it was all over; and he'd not play for her again.

Philomena smirked knowingly, eyeing Nathan up, inhaling smoke, fingering ash onto the floor as she exhaled. "S'at a fact? It's about a' ye'd expect from a bastard."

Nathan had liked Philomena. Playing with her had been good. He'd helped improve her singing, and he'd become a better-known musician. Nathan squirmed with guilt: he couldn't resist humping and sodomizing Philomena; and he couldn't handle the drinking. He was glad to be free.

Leo told him Philomena was in a bad way. She was hitting the drink and that her better gigs were drying up. Nathan regretted that she treated the gift of her voice so casually, wasting her talent when she could've done so much with it. He was sad that she'd let minor celebrity drag her down.

Nathan climbed the four stairs letting himself into the house and went to bed. To lose Dorothy because of that episode was unthinkable and as he drifted off into a shallow sleep, he murmured a half-forgotten prayer to Our Lady, begging that Dorothy would never hear about it.

Chapter Three

Nathan climbed Provident Street and turned into Galt Place. He hated Mondays and he'd worked overtime on a rush job: his legs and back ached from welding in tight spaces and corners of the submarine hull. The fumes from spent rods tainted his mouth and the tight headpiece of the hood had left him with a headache. His eyes hurt from staring through the dark glass of the hood, as he controlled the direction of the weld.

He'd bathe his eyes in soothing, cold tea. He'd not slept well and spent a restless night worrying about Dorothy. Nathan wanted to wash the sweat and dirt from his body, and rinse the foul metal taste from his mouth, before sitting down to supper with Ma. Later quiet, studying music theory and practising the Arban Method on the muted Bach.

"Nathan. Is that you?" Ma said. "Ah've a message for ye."

"Can it no' keep?"

"No. It canny keep. Dorothy's in the Royal Infirmary, she went in last night."

"Ah better get over there."

"Sit down, Nathan."

The Ward Sister had called late that afternoon. Dorothy would be in hospital for a few days. Nathan should come to the ward at two the following afternoon and ask for Sister MacKay. It would be quiet then.

Nathan bathed and felt better for it. Despite Ma's urgings, he ate little of his evening meal. He hoped Zoë might call and tell him what happened. He thought about calling her and decided against it; Zoë would tell him nothing. The lack of news made Nathan restless.

The evening stretched out ahead of him, and he went for a walk through the town, but the half hour of striding in the rain brought no relief from the worry and anxiety and he returned to Galt Place.

"Nathan. Yer making me nervous prowlin' through the house. Sit down an' content yersel. Ah'm worried as well ye know. Away an' work on yer music; practise yer trumpet."

But Nathan could not concentrate and, disgusted, threw the sheet music and the textbook to the floor. He picked up the Bach and played like an amateur, fluffing notes, botching the practice; he could not get Dorothy out of his mind.

Sleep came late and Ma shook him wake at 6.00 am. He'd slept through the alarm. He shaved, and the deep shadows under his eyes repelled him.

Ma stood over him. "You'll be in some state to see Dorothy if you don't eat yer breakfast."

That morning, Nathan worked rapidly, moving through a series of tricky jobs demanding his attention; he was glad of the variety, and for the half shift had no time to worry about Dorothy. He rushed home at noon and started worrying about Dorothy when he walked out the yard gate.

He knocked on the ward door at 2.00pm. "Can I speak to Sister MacKay, please?"

"I'm Sister MacKay. Come in."

She took Nathan to the Ward Office. Sister MacKay was about Nathan's age, attractive, prim in her starched, blue uniform, and white cap of office. She wore an engagement ring.

"I shouldn't be doing this, Mr. Forrest. You're not a relative are you?"

"I'm a friend."

Sister MacKay smiled. "Oh come on, Mr. Forrest. You're more than a friend. Miss Jones pleaded with me to get in touch with you."

"We've been going out. Is she going to be all right?"

"Dorothy has concussion and two nasty head wounds. She's a bleeder; Doctor put five stitches in the back of her head and three in her brow. She was rather bloody and confused when I admitted her. Her Aunt brought her by ambulance to Casualty on Sunday evening and said that Dorothy had fallen. There's a nasty bruise on her face and she didn't get it from a fall. I told the Aunt to leave yesterday at visiting. She shouted at Dorothy; 'I shall not tell him that you're in hospital. You're not coming back to my house unless you give him up.' Dorothy was very upset. She needs quiet."

Nathan felt like a fighter taking a battering of combination punches, leaving him stunned. He raged at Zoë, and worried about Dorothy. He rose to go into the ward and find Dorothy.

"Try to be calm, Mr. Forrest. Dorothy will be all right; she'll be here until the end of the week. We need to see that she's recovering from the concussion. Then she'll need another week to convalesce. Have you any idea what happened?"

Nathan told Sister MacKay about the disaster of Sunday evening. "Dorothy was fine when I left her at the house after our walk."

"I think the aunt hit Dorothy on the face, and it went from bad to worse. I've put a screen round her bed. You can see her now, and you'll have a bit of privacy. Try not to worry. She may be a bit weepy, but it'll pass. She will get better. We just need to keep an eye on Dorothy for a few more days. I'll get a vase for the roses."

Dorothy wasn't fully awake; she lay propped up on a heap of crisp, white pillows, the edge of a cream counterpane bordered by a white sheet rested on her breast. Her arms lay on the counter pane.

Nathan's anger vanished when he grabbed her right hand, covering her long pale, slender fingers in both of his hands. The dark blue and green-yellow bruising just above her left jaw scared him. He nearly cried when he saw the enlarged pupil of her right eye. There was a dressing lodged on her brow and the white lint of another dressing stuck out from the back of her head. Nathan wanted to strangle Zoë.

"Dorothy, Dorothy, what happened?"

"Oh, Nathan. I've got a tonsure. They shaved the back of my head. I hope I don't scar. I had a dreadful headache when I woke this morning, but it's getting better."

He wanted to hold Dorothy; to protect his love.

"Nathan, you're hurting my hand. No, no, don't let go, but don't hold it so tightly."

"Do you feel up to telling me what happened?"

"I'll try."

Dorothy intended going straight to bed. She didn't want to face another round. Zoë, however, was ready for battle.

"Zoë pounced on me in the hall, a fiend from Hell, shouting and pointing her finger. She stuck her face in mine, and I smelt the Sherry from her breath. She called you a hooligan and said she'd not permit me to see you again. I tried to get away from her and went into the kitchen, but she followed me."

"Was she drunk?" Nathan said.

"Yes, but I didn't let her off. I told her that she knew nothing of you and Ma, or the way you lived; that you'd been good and kind to me. I said that you wouldn't sink to her level of rudeness. But she wouldn't stop. She was out of control. She said, 'I know where they belong. I suppose they keep coal in the bath. No doubt, this Ma, is like my cleaning woman, worthy enough, but grubby. These people forget when to wash. My God, on the trains and buses there are flocks of them. I avoid public transport."

"Zoë called you a Catholic bastard."

"She's not the first."

"She's a wild woman. Just like my father when he's drunk."

"I see."

"I told her that she was all talk; just another notional Socialist and needed to get out from the classroom, away from her adoring young ladies, and she got all haughty: 'How dare you I am no Nazi!' "

"She's crazy."

"She hit me on the face. It really hurt. My nose tickled and salty blood came down my face and onto my blouse. I woke on the stretcher going to the ambulance. It was awful, Nathan; really horrible."

When she fainted, Dorothy fell back, and banged her head on the edge of the sink. Losing consciousness, she pitched to the right and bounced the front of her head on the kitchen bin.

"I'll have her, if she ever touches you again."

"No, Nathan. Please just stay away from her."

Dorothy looked so tired and worn out. He held onto her hand sending his love into her. "You can't go back there. Don't worry. I'll find a way."

"Time to take your leave, Mr. Forrest," Sister MacKay said. "Let Dorothy rest awhile."

"I'll see you again, very soon, Dorothy."

Sister MacKay took Nathan back to the Ward Office. "Things don't sit well with the Aunt, do they? Look Mr. Forrest, I'd like to help. If Dorothy needs a place to stay once she's convalesced, I lodge with an elderly couple; their name is Cooke and they're very nice. The house is on the other side of Lord Nelson Street. It's right in the West End. They take four girls, room and board, and no young men. They look after us. Very fair price and there's a sitting room. There's a room free from next Monday. I could ask about it for Dorothy, and I can arrange to have her things sent on."

"Thank you, thank you. Yes, please do that. When she comes out of the Infirmary, Ma and me, we'll look after her."

And so, Dorothy convalesced with Ma and Nathan. He slept in the bed settee in the sitting room and gladly surrendered his bedroom to Dorothy. Out of suffering an idyll came. Ma fussed over Dorothy; Nathan amused her, and as much as he was able, he made her laugh again. She found his records strange, and could make little of Thelonious Monk; but she liked Harry Edison a favourite horn player of Nathan's and the warm tenor of Lester Young. And Nathan wooed her with the Bach and the piano. Dorothy liked it when Nathan sang Crazy She Calls Me.

"I say I'll go through fire
And I'll go through fire
As she wants it, so it will be
Crazy she calls me
Sure, I'm crazy
Crazy in love, you see."

The song said a lot about them. Dorothy had felt heat because of Nathan. Her father hit her, and Zoë put her in the infirmary. "You put up with a lot for me, Dorothy."

Dorothy reached out, and held Nathan's hand. "I'm glad I'm here, Nathan."

Chris phoned from Prestwick Air Base, and Dorothy was touched. Leo brought his children. They sat quiet watching Dorothy sitting up in bed looking demure in the bed jacket that Ma had given her. He entertained Dorothy with tales of playing in the orchestra aboard the Queen Mary on the Southampton-New York run, and the Jazz Clubs he visited in New York.

"I went to Charlie's Tavern on Seventh Avenue, between 52nd and 53rd Streets; a great place where Jazz musicians hung out."

"How did you find it?"

"This alto player I met took me there. He knew many people. He taught me a lot. I was on the New York run for a couple of years. We went to Harlem, and I sat in. When I heard them, I realized I'd a lot to learn."

Dorothy had been staying with them for several days and looked healthier, but tired easily. He wanted her to get well and her colour to return; but he adored her pale, ivory complexion and translucent skin as she recovered.

Nathan brought the Bach to Dorothy's bedside. He caressed the trumpet, weighing it lovingly, cherishing its perfect balance, and the mellow gold finish. "I want to show you something. Would you like to get up for a little while?"

"All right."

She struggled to push herself upright. Nathan put the Bach on the dressing table, raised her, lifted the bedclothes, raised her and swung her legs over the side of the bed. Dorothy searched for her slippers, her feet pointing here and there." Hold on," he said, fitting them.

Nathan liked that the two bedrooms and the bathroom were to the back, facing the communal drying green. The sitting room and the kitchen-cum-living room faced on to Galt Place, looking over the municipal buildings and the west harbours, with good views of the river and the mountains.

The old fashioned kitchen had a dresser and a sink off set to the right of the bay window beside the pantry. A table and four upright elm chairs sat in the centre. Two easy chairs lay on either side of a glowing fireplace. A high mantle piece and dark wood surrounded the fireplace.

Nathan sat Dorothy in a chair facing the open window. She shivered in her thin dressing gown. "Wait a minute," he said, closing the window, and left the room.

Nathan returned carrying a fine, white Cashmere shawl in his outstretched hands, the long tassels swinging. He wrapped the shawl round Dorothy's shoulders, arranging the tassels on her lap. "Try that."

"It's beautiful. What is it?" Dorothy stroked the silky wool, running the tassels through her fingers.

"It's my Christening shawl."

"Why, Nathan you're blushing."

"Well, I suppose I am. I was a baby, when I wore it. But, it looks better on you than it ever did on me. A gift from Mr. Monty; he's my Godfather. Keep it; a present. It's yours, I want you to have it."

He drew the shawl closer around her shoulders. "It's a lovely present; thank you. I feel so close to you." Dorothy said.

Nathan disassembled the Bach steeping it in a basin of warm water, seasoned with mild, citrus washing soap. Using a thin, snake like brush, he swept away the deposits gathered in the horn and tuning slides. "It has to be really clean to get the tone," he said.

Nathan dried the Bach with a soft cloth, oiled the instrument, and ran the cloth through the valves and casing. He rinsed the horn with tepid running water, dried it, and oiled the tuning slide, wiping off the surplus. Nathan pushed the chair facing Dorothy closer and sat down.

"I like to give it an airing after that. It takes a few minutes. Are you tired?"

"I'm fine. I'm enjoying being up. Is the trumpet OK?"

"Yes. Just one more thing to do."

Nathan assembled the Bach, and cleaned the mouthpiece in soapy water. He pushed a spitball through the mouthpiece into the tube, blowing it through the horn a few times cleaning the inside. He oiled a fresh spitball and sent it through the horn for the last time.

The Bach looked good and smelt fresh. "Nice?" Nathan said, holding up the trumpet for her to admire.

"Play for me."

Nathan played a slow ballad. Up close to Dorothy, he felt his playing lacked polish and stopped about halfway through the song.

"Don't stop. It's a nice song."

"It's a bit rough, the trumpet on its own."

"Oh, no. I like the valves moving and your breathing. What's it called?"

Nathan sang. "I get along without you very well; Of course I do; Except when soft rains fall … from leaves,"

"I Get Along Without You Very Well. That's the name. Ach, it's a bit sentimental, but it's a nice song. I heard it first when I was in Korea; near the end; a film show at the camp, Las Vegas Story. Jane Russell and Hoagy Carmichael sang it. I kind of liked it. Sometimes we play it at a gig."

Leo heard the story in New York. Jane Brown Thompson wrote a poem and left it unsigned. Hoagy Carmichael composed the song several years after a student gave it to him. "Well, somebody found Jane Thompson but she died the night before the song was played on the radio."

"You have a good heart, Nathan. I hear it when you play."

"Not bad for a welder who plays a bit of Jazz."

"No, Nathan. You're a Jazz musician who does some welding."

With Dorothy feeling stronger, they walked from Galt Place down to the quay and the Customs House. They liked coming here. The evening sun was warm, and Nathan and Dorothy gazed across the river to the mountains. Rest, Ma's attention, and Nathan's wooing made Dorothy bloom again. Her wounds were healing. The bruise to her jaw was an unpleasant memory; the stitches in the back of her head removed the previous day. Her hair was growing over the tonsure; and the fine stitches on her brow were due for removal. Dorothy had worried about her eye, but the enlarged pupil had returned to normal.

"Have you ever wanted to leave Westburn?" Dororthy said.

"No. But I was abroad when I was in the Army."

Nathan knew people who'd moved away searching for secure work and a better life, vowing never to return. Chastened by the experience some of them came back. Talking about leaving irritated Nathan; and he hated thinking about the unknown.

"I might have left if I hadn't met Leo. The band keeps me here. And I met you. What'll we do come late September, when you go to St Andrew's?"

"I'll come home, often; some weekends." Dorothy said. "I'll want to see you. And don't forget the long holidays."

Nathan hoped that what they had would survive Dorothy's time at University. "We can be together after my class and the lesson with my teacher."

"Oh yes; and you can come up to St Andrews." Dorothy said.

"I'd not fit in with your student friends."

"Then they'd not be my friends."

He'd wait for Dorothy for he was crazy about her. She said that he made her so happy. It was hard to say how much he loved her, but he hoped she knew. He laid it out when he looked after her and it was strongest when played and sang.

"Nathan."

"Sorry. I was thinking."

It was quiet on the Quay, and Nathan cupped Dorothy's face in his hand and kissed her. Then she kissed him. "Mmm, I'm glad you stayed."

"Leo tried it," Nathan said. "A couple of years on the liner. But he missed his family and quit."

"I can see why," Dorothy said. "His wife and children are lovely."

"Leo knew this lanky kid who came to the club. He had a French name, Ronsard. Tim Ronsard, very intense. He hated Westburn and left."

"Did you work with him?"

"No. He was an apprentice fitter in Reid's Foundry just across the road from the yard."

"Oh yes. What did he do; where did he go?"

"Tim Ronsard never danced and always asked the band to play one song, My Funny Valentine; a romantic kid. Turned sixteen and had an affair with his music teacher, from school. She left Westburn, and he was low about it. She was protecting Tim. Some people in Westburn love a scandal. That's why you need to stay at the Cookes'. I'm not having any busy bodies saying anything about you."

"I know. But I wish I could stay on with Ma and you. What happened to him?"

"One night he was a little drunk and told me he was crazy about her. He called her Cliesh. He asked us to play My Funny Valentine."

"Oh, that's just lovely. But what did he do?"

"He joined the Foreign Legion. Leo told me he's a paratrooper. Jesus, Dorothy. He can't be more than eighteen, or nineteen, and he's fighting in Algeria."

"It's so sad. Was she much older?"

"About seven or eight years."

"That's like us. You're eight years older than me. I wish they'd stayed together."

"Well, I hope he's safe. I had enough soldiering in Korea."

Sunday evening. The next morning Ma would take Dorothy to the Cookes' by taxi. Nathan started work down the yard at 7.30 in the morning and would not be with them. It was late, and Ma came into Nathan's room. He was sitting by the piano; Dorothy sitting nearby.

Ma seemed awkward. "Ah don't know how yer placed Dorothy, but here, take this," she said, handing Dorothy a folded envelope.

Nathan tinkered with the keyboard, sending quiet ripples of Just You, Just Me, into the corners of the room.

"What is it, Ma?"

"Somethin' to tide ye over. Ye'll have expense an' things at the Cookes'."

"Oh, Ma, that's so kind and thoughtful of you. But honestly, I'm all right. My mother left me a bank account, and I draw on it."

"Ye never know, ye might need it. Hang on to it." It was the cementing of a great friendship between Dorothy and Ma.

"Dorothy, will ye come wi' me to Glasgow; help me wi' the messages?"

"Yes; of course, Ma."

Mr. Monty was coming for the weekend and Ma was shopping at the Kosher grocer and butcher in Glasgow. Dorothy watched Ma pick treats to please Mr. Monty: the rose jam, blintzes stuffed with raisins; Odessa food. Ma, chatting to the Kosher butcher, inspecting the row of chickens. Ma selected a large plump bird. Chris was coming too on Saturday night.

Ma par boiled the chicken to make soup; and later added kreplach. "Ye can help me make it, if ye like, Dorothy."

"I'd like to try, Ma."

Galt Place, mid afternoon, leg-tired and footsore after a morning walking on hard pavements, Ma and Dorothy prepared the dinner for next day. Ma made dough of flour and eggs, rolling it into thin sheets, cutting the sheets into small squares.

"Ah stuff the kreplach wi' fine-chopped white meat, add salt, pepper, and onions. Then Ah roll the edges of the dough together, firm like, an' they go into the soup. It's tasty. Nathan likes it."

Dorothy worked alongside Ma, and soon there was an orderly heap of kreplach at her side of the dresser.

"That's perfect, Dorothy. After the soup, Ah think we'll have Prune Chicken."

"Prunes, Ma?"

"Don't you worry, Dorothy. Ah've been makin' it for while now an' it's good."

Ma made a sauce from fresh tomatoes. With deft incisions of an old and sharp kitchen knife, she skinned the chicken, cut it into neat portions, coating them with flour, seasoning with salt, and pepper. The chicken pieces arranged in a dish, layered with sliced onions and decorated with prunes. Ma covered the chicken in tomato sauce. It was ready for baking in the oven.

For dessert Ma made teiglach. "The dough's mixed with sugar, and ginger; then Ah roll it into wee balls and fry them in honey."

"Can I help, Ma?"

"Sure Dorothy. You'll like the teiglach."

"What kind of wine is that?" Dorothy said.

"Mevushal wine. Mr. Monty likes it. An' we can have a glass as well."

"Does Nathan ever have wine?"

"No, Dorothy; an' it's better that way: he never takes a drink."

"I understand, Ma."

They tidied the kitchen. "What's Mr. Monty like?" Dorothy said.

"Well, Ah found him a wee bit strange at first."

The owner showed Montague Solomon round the pawn and announced that he'd bought the business. Mr. Solomon's star lighted the drab work area. He seemed older in his dark, well-cut overcoat and brilliant white shirt with the hard collar; the rich silk tie lightened his appearance. His quick eyes, suggesting an enigmatic nature both shrewd and amusing, missed nothing.

Ma didn't like him, and though she'd served an apprenticeship in the pawn, and was now supervisor, decided to give notice.

"Ah'd never met anybody like him. Ah'd served ma time in the pawn and ah wis the supervisor but Ah meant to leave. Ah wis sure he'd sack me."

"Why, Ma?"

"Tae tell the truth, Dorothy, Ah wis afraid of him. But Ah wis wrong. He's a nice man, a good man."

"Mrs. Forrest, I can see that you're afraid of me. There's no need. I apologise for causing you to feel put out. Please stay on. Together we can make this a good business."

"He swayed me, Dorothy, an'Ah stayed."

The pawn continued to deal with clothing and bedding, but branched out, strengthening the business in jewellry and watches, drawing on Ma's talent for evaluating precious stones, and Mr. Montague's deft work with watches, diamonds, and precious metals.

He'd never liked the formal Mr. Solomon, and thought Ma was teasing, when she called him Mr. Monty. But he saw her affectionate respect and liked his new name. They worked well together, and a friendship blossomed.

Mr. Monty lived in Westburn for many years and had a few friends among its small Jewish community; he belonged to the place where he made a living. There was mutual liking and respect between him and Ma: she invited him to Galt Place. Knowing that he was Kosher, Ma learned to prepare suitable food. Soon, Mr. Monty and the Forrests were friends.

When Nathan's mother died, Mr. Monty was there with a quiet word and practical support. He was disappointed at the Parish Priest's attempt to remove Nathan from Ma and James' care. For several months, Mr. Monty paid Ma's wages while she nursed Nathan, until James could look after him.

"James, ma husband, wis in a bad way after the Army," Ma said. "The mustard gas wrecked his lungs. The Army pension wis a pittance an' Ah wis the wage earner."

"I see," Dorothy said.

"Ye know about Nathan's mum, Dorothy?"

"Yes, Ma. Nathan told me."

"We were friends with Mr. Monty when Nathan was born, but Ah never expected what he did for us. The Parish Priest wis cruel tryin' to take Nathan away. James put him out of the house. Ah don't know that we'd have managed without Mr. Monty."

Ma made a pot of tea and laid out cups and saucers, sugar and milk. "A tea biscuit, Dorothy?"

"Oh yes, Ma."

Ma poured the tea. "There's a sadness about Mr. Monty at times."

"Why, Ma; what happened?"

"Well, he was great with a woman here in Westburn; a Gentile; a Presbyterian."

"What was she like; how did he meet her?"

"Prim. He met her through the pawn, but she was a nice lassie when ye got to know her."

Mr. Monty kept meticulous accounts for the pawn and chose a Westburn accounting firm with an unblemished reputation to audit the books. The Head Bookkeeper was a youngish woman, Flora Nash, past thirty and unmarried. To Westburn eyes, she was a Matron on the threshold of spinsterhood. Mr. Monty had several meetings with Miss Nash and found himself looking forward to seeing her.

Mr. Monty dressed elegantly in fine garments of subdued grey, blue, and brown wool cloth; well cut double breasted suits, brilliant white shirts with a glosssy hard collar, and at his throat a well-knotted gaily coloured tie. Ma felt that his appearance added class to the pawn. Mr. Monty's Cologne brightened the pawn. "He had a nice smell," Ma said.

When he was due at the accountants, Mr. Monty struck a note of heightened elegance; the incisive crease in his trousers, the dazzling polish of his shoes, and the change to sober, solid coloured ties suggesting reliability.

"Ma," Mr. Monty said. "That Knoxian mask hides a good looking woman. I'd like to know Flora Nash."

Ma met Flora Nash when she brought papers to the pawn. Miss Nash was the image of the douce Presbyterian, attached to the Kirk, and her profession. The gap between Flora Nash and Westburn's Catholics was vast enough; but an abyss separated her from Mr. Monty.

One Sunday morning when the Protestant churches emptied, Mr. Monty walked on The Esplanade in the West End, not far from where he lived, and met Miss Nash. She too walked enjoying the views of the river and the mountains. She was a year or two younger than he, and in her modestly heeled shoes almost as tall. She was so pretty in her cloche hat and fitting autumn coat, clutching a brown leather hand bag to her side. Mr. Monty swept off his fedora and saluted Flora Nash, standing aside to let her pass.

"Good afternoon, Miss Nash."

A blush and her neck and face were a pretty pink. Miss Nash's dark myopic eyes, magnified behind small rimless glasses, lit and her Knoxian mask vanished in a smile of recognition, making Mr. Monty very happy.

Ma worried about Mr. Monty and asked about Flora Nash. Miss Nash was thirty-two and lived alone in a small Edwardian villa. She was an only child born late to her parents who'd died in their early sixties. The word among local business folk was that Miss Nash enjoyed a moderate roughness; she was comfortable.

Mr. Monty telephoned Flora Nash from the pawn and invited her to tea at his flat the following Sunday afternoon. There would be two other guests.

Ma and James Forrest, Nathan in his pram, walked through the West End to Mr. Monty's plain but comfortable flat on The Esplanade. They arrived before Flora Nash so that Ma could help prepare tea.

Miss Nash was formal; a brief pressing of hands and a murmured, "How do you do?" She recognized Ma from the pawn.

Nathan fretted and Ma heated a bottle for him but he wailed and would not be still. Mr. Monty hovered above Ma and tickled Nathan with his fore finger; Nathan cried loudly. "I'm Nathan's Godfather, you know," he said turning to Miss Nash, "I've upset him."

"Can I try, Mrs. Forrest," Miss Nash said. "You don't mind?"

"No, no, Miss Nash; not at all."

Miss Nash cradled Nathan in her left arm, coaxing him with the bottle in her right hand. Ma worried that he'd foul his nappy or break wind. Nathan took the bottle and sucked contentedly. "Nathan; such a nice name. He's a lovely boy."

"But what happened, Ma," Dorothy said. "Why didn't they marry?"

"Everything went well at first."

Mr. Monty went away for weekends with Miss Nash to quiet places, far from the prying eyes of Westburn, and Ma guessed that they'd become lovers. She offered prayers to St Christopher to keep the lovers safe in their travels.

Mr. Monty, Jewish, and Flora Nash, a Protestant. He would not convert to her faith and did not expect Flora to become Jewish, a difficult undertaking. His parents would have preferred it had he met a nice Jewish girl, but they raised no objections.

Until she fell in love Flora Nash had resigned herself to the solitary life, ignored by the tasteless blades of Westburn. Happily she accepted Mr. Monty's proposal and his suggestion that they marry at a civil ceremony leaving them free to worship, and raise their children in the Jewish faith.

"But what happened, Ma?"

"They'd just got engaged. A reckless driver mounted the pavement and ran her over. She was dead when the ambulance brought her to the Infirmary."

It was a man from Flora Nash's side of Westburn killed her, a Valentian returning from a liquid lunch. He got off with a heavy fine and a suspended sentence when the case came to Court.

"Mr. Monty was in a terrible state; wasn't himself for months. He never met another woman and that's a pity."

"Gosh, Ma. That must have been awful. I'm so sorry."

"Don't you worry, Dorothy, ye'll like him. Mr. Monty's great company. When he comes by train, he likes Nathan tae meet him at the station. Ye can go with him if ye like."

A tall man with smooth features and well into his middle years got down from the first-class carriage. He stood out from the other passengers. Mr. Monty was rather grave in a black fedora and dark conservative clothes; horn-rimmed glasses suggested a scholar or a rabbi, but not a pawnbroker who loved Jazz and delighted in the company of his friends. He put down his weekend case and scanned the people waiting on the platform; he smiled and waved when he saw Nathan and Dorothy.

"Hello, Nathan," he said embracing him affectionately, and then turning to Dorothy. "You must be Dorothy, I'm so pleased to meet you at last." he said, grasping Dorothy's hand.

After refreshments of tea and assorted biscuits and himself settled at Galt Place, Mr. Monty knew that Ma needed time on her own to finish the preparations for dinner.

"Let's go for a stroll," Mr. Monty said. "Later we might sit in the park. It's a fine afternoon and it's been a while since I had a look around Westburn."

They strolled eastwards along Cathcart Street. "You like gardening, Dorothy?"

"Yes, I do. I used to help my Ayah in Hong Kong. Our garden in Calle Crescent is lovely. My Mum loves working in the garden."

"Look," Mr. Monty said. "See the wild garden?"

"Gosh," Dorothy said. "Its just lovely." She caught Nathan's hand as he cast a lazy glance at the bomb site. Dorothy dragged Nathan across the street and Mr. Monty followed.

The scars of the Blitz softened and from the crumbling bricks Dorothy snatched a Dahlia that had flourished against the odds, from a meagre clump that rose over a splash of pansies and verdant disorder of weeds. A floral display that had survived in this postage stamp of hard earth. She held the yellow petals under Nathan's nose, and he sneezed.

"It's quite nice," he said, tucking his handkerchief into his sleeve.

"Nathan," Dorothy said. "Don't you see; these gorgeous flowers are a sign of hope?"

"Dorothy's right," Mr. Monty said. "Good families used to live here in solid tenements before the Blitz. I hope one day they'll come back."

Mr. Monty urged Nathan and Dorothy on farther east, stopping at the tugboats moored two deep to the quayside. "I love the Docks; there's a trace yet of Westburn's glory days."

They stood at the dry dock gate, on the eastern boundary of the Victoria Harbour. Mr. Monty lingered, gazing at the trim new frigate, resting on blocks, her hull exposed in the dry dock. She was in the last stages of fitting out, and about ready for sea trials.

"Look at the lines: perfect symmetry," Mr. Monty said.

They gazed at the elegant sweep of the bows, the sugar loaf for'ard turret mounting the twin 4.5-inch guns, the unobtrusive stack, sheltered by a slim lattice mast soaring above the bridge and surrounding super structure; the hull tapering to the square stern and the dry dock gate.

"There's talent in Westburn," Mr. Monty said. "That's a bonny frigate."

The yard belonged to the elite that built naval ships, bringing honour to the town, and the gifted men who created the beautiful Men of War; their skills and enterprise bound the community of Westburn. If the naval work vanished Westburn would decline further.

They walked on, passing the stocks to the last slipway, looking up at the part-built hull of a merchantman, casting a shadow over the yard gate. The yards would not collapse this year, perhaps not in five years, but ten years? Mr. Monty could not see a new generation of leadership emerging in the yards or in the community to reverse the decline and restore Westburn's glory.

"It can't last, Nathan. I don't see another frigate on the stocks. Will there be more naval work? Look at the empty stocks. Where's the orders for new merchant ships; what'll happen to the skilled men if the orders don't come; what'll happen to Westburn when the orders for merchant ships go to Japan?"

Nathan shrugged, and Dorothy looked from Nathan to Mr. Monty who caught her arm and hurried on. "I want to show you something."

They stood just inside the dock gates. Built in the 1880s by confident investors it had been one of the largest enclosed docks in the world, receiving cargoes of sugar and tobacco, but was surpassed by the enclosed docks at Liverpool and elsewhere. The narrow footbridge mounting the dock gates holding back the tide led to an imposing villa, Garvel House, built in the late 18th century, now marooned on what had once been land above the high water mark.

They gazed on the villa, its fine honey sandstone walls blackened, the windows boarded up and the doors battened down. Loose slates littered the roof.

"Westburn should be proud of that house," Mr. Monty said. "The man who built it had confidence in the future; he did something good. Look at it now: what a sorry state: all sooty stains and crumbling sandstone and cruelly neglected. I believe the town is ashamed of it. One of these days it'll be demolished."

"Oh I hope not," Dorothy said. "It's so beautifully proportioned."

"You know, Dorothy," Mr. Monty said. "A lack of confidence will ruin Westburn."

Nathan gave a passing thought to Mr. Monty's concerns and Dorothy's hopes for the house: he acknowledged Westburn's indifference to beautiful buildings, and the capacity of politicians to erase them. But the thought soon vanished, for Nathan had found beauty in Jazz, and in Dorothy he had discovered love.

Nathan ignored his unsteady collapsing milieu, and concentrated on perfecting his playing. But deep anchors moored Nathan to Westburn: he felt responsible for Ma. Mr. Monty wasn't getting any younger and had no close relatives in Scotland. Nathan's affection for Mr. Monty went far beyond liking: he admired him and loved him for his kindness and wisdom. If he were ever ill or infirm, Nathan would take care of him.

"Mr. Monty," Nathan said. "Tell Dorothy about Odessa. She's dying to hear about it."

"Nathan," Dorothy said.

"Oh that's all right, Dorothy, I like to ramble about the past."

Nathan knew the story that brought the Solomons to Scotland. Life was hard; Nathan was proud that ten thousand Jews had settled in Glasgow. He never tired of hearing Mr. Monty's story; had heard it so often he could tell it himself. Mr. Monty had shaped Nathan. The Solomon story had influenced Nathan and Ma; they were part of the narrative.

"Ah, Odessa," Mr. Monty said. "Tiny spoonfuls of the sweetest rose jam; and the tieglach."

"Oh, there's rose jam, and there's raisin filled blintzes," Dorothy said. "I helped Ma with the shopping. And she let me make tieglach."

"Good, good," Mr. Monty said. "And blintzes. Already I'm hungry."

Mr. Monty's childhood memories piled up. "The Steps, the Richelieu Stairs; that's what they used to be called. Now they're The Potemkin. Such fun for a small boy scampering up and down. I used to go there with my mother and father," he said, showing worn teeth in a broad smile. "Sometimes, I fell down, and cried for my bruised knees. Then my mother would pick me up. I can just remember the terraces of trees on each side, and the sweep of tall buildings at the top of the stairs. Aach; it was a lifetime ago. I was just five when we left."

Mr. Monty liked living in Scotland; was happy to be British and from his father he learnt that Scotland was the only European country with no history of state persecution of his people.

"My father used to get homesick for the warm Odessa summers. But he felt safe in Scotland. There were no pogroms here. That's one of the reasons we left the old country; and the uncertainty. What was it, Bailik said, 'the slaughter came with the spring.' Odessa could be a cruel and dismal place."

Mr. Monty reminisced about the early years in Scotland: his father finding work as a furrier, his mother looking after the rented tenement flat with outside jakes, set in beds, a cast iron sink, with a brass swan neck tap. Water heated on the black cast iron range. His sister was born in Glasgow in 1900; she died in the epidemic of Spanish flu in 1919. His father was a hard working furrier; after a few years he opened his own business. The word of his skill spread, and slowly the family prospered. By 1913 they had moved to a well-appointed tenement apartment on the southwest side of the city. But to the end of his working life, the father kept his business premises in the Gorbals.

Mr. Monty was the keeper of the family memories.

The afternoon light weakened: the sun over the Argyll Hills; it was a good walk back to Ma's. "Shall we make a start?" Mr. Monty said. "I'd like to sit in the Well Park before we go in."

They retraced their steps until they passed the frigate. Mr. Monty turned to take the high road. He forced a steady pace on Nathan and Dorothy. He pointed to a drab two storey building with grey rough cast walls and small windows in Terrace Road, the Labour Exchange.

"The unemployed register in there," Mr. Monty said. "They call it 'The Buroo.' May God keep you from it, Nathan."

They stopped at the wrought iron gates of the Well Park. "Fine work," Mr. Monty said. "I like to see something that's well done."

They sat on a bench facing west; sunlight filtered through the branches of oak and plane trees. "I like the park," Dorothy said. "Nathan brought me here when we first met."

"I like it too," Mr. Monty said.

Mr. Monty stared at the imposing war memorial. "Were you in the war?" Dorothy said.

"Yes; not the last one, though I did war work as a tool maker, and Ma ran the pawn while I was away. I joined the Army in 1915. I volunteered."

It was difficult for Dorothy to imagine this elderly, avuncular man, as a tall, well-built twenty-year old in the Highland Light Infantry who'd served with honour in Flanders.

Mr. Monty researched the origins of pawnbroking, deciding that it was an honourable calling.

"I was glad to get home, Dorothy. After the Army, I was unsettled, but I came to like my business. Some people, Dorothy, look down on pawnbrokers. Ma and myself, well, we provided a service. We helped people when they had no where else to turn."

"I think so," Dorothy said.

"Pawn, has Latin roots," Mr. Monty said: "patinum; it means cloth or clothing; hence, the pawnshop. The symbol of the three balls is a link to the Medicis and other Florentine families. They sometimes modified the balls to orbs, plates and discs and coin as evidence of their wealth and success."

"I see," Dorothy said.

"The Medicis established links with the Lombard bankers in London; that was in the late Middle Ages. The light of respectability has shone on pawnbrokers down the centuries."

"You have to tell Dorothy more," Nathan said.

"I was a terrible boy," Mr. Monty said. "I was near my full height at fourteen; all arms and legs, pinched face. I kept shooting out of my clothes. I must have been a sorry sight when I was apprenticed to a pawnbroker, a friend of my father's."

"Did you want to become a pawnbroker?" Dorothy said.

"I never thought about it, Dorothy. My father sent me. He was a good man, the pawnbroker. I learned a lot by just watching and listening to him."

Mr. Monty learnt from this wise man a way of business and how to live and deal with customers. His first uncertain steps, valuing clothing and bedding. Gradually increased responsibilities developed his judgement valuing jewellery, diamond rings, and watches. Mr. Monty always lent at a fair rate of interest. He acquired a firm sympathy for the Gorbals' inhabitants, knowing when to refuse loans on goods brought by suspicious people or known crooks. He protected the good name of the pawn, avoiding trouble with the police, the contempt of his own people and customers.

In quiet periods and working in the evening after the pawn closed, Mr. Monty immersed himself in watch making, repairing jewellery, working in gold, and silver. He had a fine eye and delicate hands. His polite and exact Glasgow accent endeared him to his customers. When he was nineteen, Mr. Monty had a well balanced understanding of the people of the Gorbals and the importance of pawnbroking.

"Generally people were friendly. But, when I refused a loan, some people called me Sheeny."

"That's so unpleasant," Dorothy said.

"Yes, Dorothy, but it was a mild epithet, light years away from the pogroms of Odessa."

Mr. Monty got on well with his customers, good folk, a mix of feckless Irish Catholics and dour Protestant boozers, many of the latter with ties to the Orange Order. He never bored, or made them impatient with asides about his profession. It was his duty to give them a swift decision on a loan against their property.

"If they were glum, Dorothy, or querulous, I'd tell the Irish that St Nicholas was the patron saint of pawnbrokers. The Orangemen liked knowing that Stone of Destiny was Jacob's pillow stone."

"The Stone of Destiny, kept at Scone?" Dorothy said.

"That's the one, for the crowning of the Kings of Scotland," Mr. Monty said. "And the English stole it."

They sat quiet enjoying the sweet breezes rippling through the trees, cooling the heat of the late afternoon sun. Mr. Monty had never seen Nathan so happy: Dorothy was a fine, and rather beautiful girl, and that afternoon she was in looks. It was clear to him that Nathan was very much in love. He could see it in the way he walked by her side. Though Dorothy was fit and healthy, Nathan waited on her, assisting her across roads and walking so that she was on the inside of the pavement. It delighted Mr. Monty to see Nathan being gallant. And it pleased him that Dorothy returned Nathan's affection.

The warm sun and his proximity to Westburn's war memorial lured Mr. Monty farther into memory. He loved Scotland; he was patriotic and felt Scottish; had joined Glasgow's own regiment and served honourably in Flanders. That he was a Jew born in Odessa, meant that Mr. Monty was even handed with Protestants and Irish Catholics. In the HLI, Mr. Monty had served with men of both religions. But in basic training, the men asked whether he was a Rangers Jew or Celtic Jew. It was a test to find out whose side he was on; was he for the Blue or the Green? Wisely, he said neither: he was simply a Jew. At the Front, the tension between Protestants and Catholics vanished as men fought and died in the trenches.

Mr. Monty sighed, remembering the ambiguous, prejudiced whispers against Catholics in the yards and engineering foundries of Westburn. He regretted the hostility separating the two communities. In civilian life, it would have been folly to take sides.

He'd witnessed the havoc that arrogant priests could wreak on their flock and remembered the bad time Ma and James Forrest had when Nathan was born and his mother died.

Ma invited Mr. Monty to see the new baby. He liked the name: Nathan, a Gift from God; a good name for a boy born out of wedlock, his mother dead. Mr. Monty brought a parcel for Nathan's layette. Mr. Monty's mother knitted a pair of woollen boots, matching mitts, a tiny cardigan, a cap to protect the boy's head from Westburn's winds. And the shawl; the Cashmere shawl that had belonged to his sister who'd died from Spanish flu in 1919. Mr. Monty was proud of the beautiful shawl of the finest white wool with long silken tassels hanging from the ends.

When he arrived at Galt Place the Parish Priest sat in the kitchen with Ma and James. The atmosphere was tense. Father Thomas Reilly, a burly well fed Irishman in late middle age, did not get up when Ma introduced Mr. Monty; he grunted.

"Like I told ye, Forrest," Reilly said. "Yez are better givin' him up now. I'll take him away the day and have him in a good and daecent Catholic family, to a loving married couple by tonight. Yez'll thank me fur this mercy in years to come."

"My daughter just died giving birth," James said. "We buried her from your church."

Mr. Monty rose. "I'll come back in an hour."

"I'd like you to stay," Ma said.

James stood; his lungs, damaged by mustard gas in the War troubled him and he did not look well. "Sit down Mr. Monty. We invited you. You're always welcome here. This one," and he turned to the Priest, "barged his way in." Reilly's eyebrows shot up.

"Get out, Reilly, before Ah throw ye doon the bloody stairs" James said. "Don't come here again."

Reilly got out of the chair, his face flushed. Mr. Monty wondered where Reilly had spent the years 1914-1918, when James served in France. Mr. Monty got up ready to eject the priest if he touched James.

"Damn ye, Forrest," Reilly said. "I'm offerin' yez a chance to wipe out that boy's bastardy. Ye'll live to regret this day."

"This way," Mr. Monty said. He gripped Reilly's elbow and showed him the door.

Ma recovered and James calmed down. James got up, put on the kettle, and made a pot of tea. By the second cup they were all in a better mood and Mr. Monty handed the parcel to Ma. The Cashmere shawl delighted her and she ran the long silken tassels through her fingers and pressed the shawl to her cheek.

"Isn't it lovely, James?" Ma said running the long silken tassels through her fingers.

"It certainly is," James said.

Ma placed the shawl carefully on the top of the sideboard, and kissed Mr. Monty on the cheek. "Thank you so much, Mr. Monty. We'll always treasure these gifts."

"Millie, we'll baptize Nathan, here in the house this afternoon," James said. "Ah'll never ask that swine Reilly fur anything."

Westburn Catholics believed that the souls of dead unbaptized babies have the stain of Original Sin and cannot enter Heaven. God keeps their souls in Limbo. So in Westburn, Catholics baptized soon after birth.

Ma had purchased a fine silk gown for the Baptism and she went to the bedroom to get it. She picked Nathan up from the clothing basket where he lay on a thick quilt and had slept through the row with the Priest, a tiny precious bundle wrapped in a white sheet and warm blanket. Ma washed his face with a soft cloth, waking him, and he gazed unfocussed. She removed his sleeping garments, dressed him in his finery and combed his wisp of hair.

"I'd like to wrap him in the shawl, Mr. Monty. Is that all right?"

"Why of course, of course. I'm honoured."

"Will you be his Godfather?" James said to Mr. Monty, and Ma nodded in agreement.

"I'd like that very much."

James Forrest knew nothing of Catholic theology, but in his intermittent practice of the Faith had picked up knowledge of the ceremonies affecting families; he knew enough of the ritual to baptize his grandson. He poured clean tap water into a mixing bowl, and though it was not required, he trusted the efficacy of Westburn superstition: James dropped a pinch of salt in the bowl of water and made the Sign of the Cross over it. He did not know that the Church frowned on Non Catholics acting as sponsor. It did not concern him that a twisted priest like Reilly might rule that the ceremony he was about to conduct was invalid. Mr. Monty was a good man and James Forrest possessed a simple faith, that in God's eyes he'd chosen well, in asking him to be Nathan's witness and his Godfather. James's intentions were Holy and he would bring Nathan up a Catholic.

Ma drew the Cashmere shawl back from Nathan's head to the edge of his shoulders. She stroked the fine silk of the gown, and handed him to James who cradled Nathan in the crook of his left arm.

"Nathan, I Baptize thee in the name of the Father," and made the first pouring from his cupped hand; he dipped into the bowl of water, "the Son," and made the second pouring; dipping again into the bowl, slightly jarred by Nathan's gurgling protests at the water falling on his face, "and the Holy Ghost," and made the third pouring. He handed Nathan back to Ma who dabbed his face dry and rearranged the Cashmere shawl.

When Nathan was asleep, James brought out a bottle of Johnnie Walker Black Label, and three glasses, pouring a measure into each one. He raised his glass and Ma and Mr. Monty raised their glasses. "Tae Nathan; may he have a good life," James said.

But Reilly's behaviour left Ma embittered and she stopped going to Mass. Of course, her attachment to Catholicism ran deeper than her anger, and the Church's principles guided Ma's life: she brought Nathan up in the Faith and sent him to a Catholic school. To have sent Nathan to a Protestant school was unthinkable. Mr. Monty was disgusted when an asinine School Chaplain taunted Nathan about his illegitimacy, driving him away from the Church.

A blessing of their alienation from the Church was Ma and Nathan's lack of prejudice, and they stood back from the frictions plaguing their neighbours.

Ma liked Dorothy and was unconcerned that she was not Catholic. Mr. Monty jaloused that Dorothy's father, a man attached to drink and troubled by disappointment at work, would object to Nathan because he was a Catholic and a working man. Hanging over Dorothy was the difficult situation with the explosive and violent Zoë, who loathed Catholics. Mr. Monty wondered what hand fate held for Nathan and Dorothy, and prayed for a happier outcome than his own thwarted love.

If only his beloved Flora had lived, her parents from Odessa or Lvov, and Nathan was their son, and Dorothy was a nice Jewish girl, her grandparents from Kracow. How much brighter life in Scotland might have looked for them.

"Mr. Monty, Mr. Monty," Dorothy said. "Are you all right?" Her hand touching his shoulder, roused him.

"Ah, ah… I'm fine Dorothy. I must have dropped off. Did I tell you that I live in Newton Mearns?" He laughed. "The train from Glasgow; it's called the Palestine Express."

Ma was content as she looked round the table; the meal had gone well. She smiled at Dorothy: for a wee slip of a thing, Dorothy had a healthy appetite, and despite her earlier misgivings about prunes, Mr. Monty easily persuaded her to have a second helping of chicken.

Nathan was glad that Mr. Monty liked Dorothy. At dinner, Mr. Monty kept her glass brimming with meshuval wine.

Chris had brought a bottle of Maker's Mark for Mr. Monty, and he opened it after dinner. Ma produced small glasses and they moved to the Good Room. "Sipping whisky, from Kentucky," Chris said.

Nathan shook his head at the offer of a shot. Not that he'd worried about Dorothy drinking too much, but he noticed the flush on her face brought on by the meshuval wine, and he was glad when she held the palm of her hand above the small glass. "No thank you, Mr. Monty."

Mr. Monty was garrulous as the meshuval wine and the Maker's Mark released an aquifer of memory. He was glad when the War ended, and he left tool making and returned to his pawn broking business. He was cheered by the founding of Israel and, if he'd been younger, would have gone there to take part in the War of Independence. But he did what he could, and sent funds.

One evening as they closed the pawn, he said to Ma. "Israel; a country for Jews. You know Ma, justice at last; and a refuge from the horrors of Europe."

But the wartime austerities continued and darkened the early years of the peace. By 1948 Mr. Monty was fed up with food rationing, the pinched faces of hungry Scots, and the shabbiness of life. Ma worried that he might fall ill. But knowing of his love of the music, and that he had cousins in New York, suggested he made the effort to get away. So, he'd overcome the difficulties of postwar travel and arranged to visit and to soak up Jazz.

"Dorothy, Chris, let me tell you about my fling in New York."

It was an extravagant pilgrimage: he wished he'd been a younger man and not too old for a Zoot suit. But when he arrived in the City, he bought a drape jacket of fine red wool, and black slacks with pinched bottoms, a white shirt with a deep rolled collar and a loud tie.

"A futile attempt at being Hip. I was an embarrassment to my cousins. I kept the tie. It's still there in the back of my wardrobe, but the rest of the outfit I left in New York. I could never have worn it here."

"Oh that's too bad," Dorothy said.

"Ma ran the pawn while I was away. Nathan helped Ma in the evenings and worked in the pawn at weekends."

"You were a pawnbroker, Nathan?" Dorothy said.

"Not really. I worked at moving and storing things, and I helped Ma with a stocktaking. Ma and Mr. Monty wanted me to come into the business, but I didn't fancy it."

Ma and Mr. Monty would have made Nathan a great pawnbroker, but he was headstrong. Nathan wanted to work with his hands. And he'd picked up the view in school, that pawning property was shameful.

Mr. Monty had a word with a yard foreman who bought jewellery, and secured a welding apprenticeship for Nathan.

"New York; it was one of my great experiences, Dorothy. It was so exciting. I don't think I've had as much fun in my life. I went to Minton's to hear Monk, Howard McGhee, and Roy Eldgridge. I saw Charlie Parker and Dizzy Gillespie in Carnegie Hall."

"You really heard them?" Chris said.

"Yes, Chris. I'll never forget it."

"I've heard Monk. Nathan has some of his records," Dorothy said. "I didn't understand it."

"Sometime we'll play him, Dorothy," Chris said.

"I'm glad I went. I love Jazz," Mr. Monty said.

"It sounds wonderful," Dorothy said. "Nathan told me that you introduced him to Jazz."

"Chris, Nathan," Mr. Monty said. "Play something by Gershwin." The band was rehearsing the next afternoon for the forthcoming Jazz Festival, and Chris had brought his tenor.

Ma excused herself, and went to the kitchen to wash up.

"This might sound a bit rough," Nathan said. He exchanged a look with Chris. They preferred to play with bass and drums.

Chris sounded a flurry of notes from his tenor. Nathan picked up the Bach, fingered the valves and fitted a mute to the bell; he nodded to Chris. "You ready, Mr. Monty?"

"Yes, yes, I'm really looking forward to this."

They began with Eddie Durham's Topsy, and it was a bit rough; an uncertain start as they searched for a grip of the song: Nathan's rasping breath, the clip-clipping of the tenor's key pads, as Chris' fingers found the tempo; and they clicked. The playing was not loud, but it was intense, and swung. Their controlled breathing, the shared intuition: two musicians who understood each other's tricks and nuances. Nathan removed the mute and blew a staccato stream of notes, paused and blew again; two well aimed salvoes: variants on the tune, encouraging Chris' improvised plunder. They finished handing eight bar solos back and forth.

They played for an hour, taking Dorothy and Mr. Monty to hidden places in the songs. At times they lost Dorothy, but always Mr. Monty was on their heels. After four songs, Chris let the tenor hang from its sling and Nathan's right arm hung slack, holding the Bach.

"One more?" Chris said.

Nathan raised the Bach to his lips and puffed out a flurry of exploratory notes. Chris blew hard, patterns of honks and squeaks from the tenor, confusing Mr. Monty.They fooled around, creating false Gershwin starts, puzzling Dorothy and teasing Mr. Monty. Gradually they settled down, shoulders moving rhythmically to their feet tapping on the lino as they settled on mid tempo for a swinging version of Love Walked In.

They finished, grinning, bowing to Dorothy and Mr. Monty's applause, laying aside the trumpet, and the tenor sax, pleased at what they'd done.

"I liked that very much," Dorothy said.

"Wonderful, wonderful," Mr. Monty said. "Thank you, Chris and Nathan." The playing had been perfect. Nathan was in love, and with Dorothy there, his playing was deep and intense, and often tender. Chris played beautifully.

"Excuse me," Dorothy said. When she came back Dorothy had the Cashmere shawl round her shoulders. The room was cool.

"Nice shawl, Dorothy," Mr. Monty said.

"Thank you. You don't mind that I'm wearing it? I know you gave it for Nathan's Baptism."

"Of course not. You know I'm Nathan's Godfather?"

"Yes; he told me."

The shawl, and Mr. Monty's thoughts turned to Flora Nash. A love match of a Jew and a Gentile, then a drunk driver killed Flora.

He thought about the likely opposition of Dorothy's parents to Nathan and the hatred of Zoë for Nathan and for Catholics. Mr. Monty had seen the heartache caused by Protestant-Catholic loathing: broken engagements, falling outs at Baptisms and weddings. He prayed that Nathan and Dorothy would not be poisoned by her family's prejudice.

But he felt optimistic: Nathan had grown up in a world of Catholic and Protestant antagonisms and rejected it; Ma was the most tolerant person; and Dorothy, innocent and idealistic, brought up in Hong Kong, educated at Public School, was untouched by it. There was hope for them.

Mr. Monty sipped from his glass of Maker's Mark. "Dorothy, you know Nathan is a wooden Catholic? He's a timber Tim."

"I'm sorry, Mr. Monty; I don't know what you mean."

"Nathan doesn't practise the Faith; doesn't attend to his duties, do you understand why?"

"Ah, I see; and yes, I think so."

"And he's a better Jazz musician for it. Otherwise, he'd be chained to the Silver Band and Irishness."

"Really," Dorothy said.

Nathan had looked out, and ascended from the silver band to Jazz musician. When Leo introduced him to Chris, Nathan and the band moved forward, drawing on Chris' people: Armstrong, Hawkins, Webster, Parker, and many more. When Nathan played, he soared above Westburn.

"What inspiration," Mr. Monty said. "It's unusual the way an American musician and Scots musicians come together. Chris is quite exceptional."

Dorothy nodded eagerly, suspecting that Mr. Monty was tipsy, and not quite sure what to make of his remarks.

Dorothy's presence and the drink had loosened Mr. Monty's tongue. "When they play," he said."I hear the blues, and the foundries and the shipyards. The music has verve."

"I see," Dorothy said. Chris shifted awkwardly in his seat as he dried his tenor. She worried that the day might end badly.

"Ah don't have any fancy ideas about the music," Nathan said. "Ah rely on the song, only the song."

"Yes, I see what you mean," Dorothy said.

"We're good," Nathan said. "But I don't think we're that good."

"Well, the band could get better," Mr. Monty said. "That means getting away from Westburn. Lift the band to a higher level of artistry. Change, risk, imagination. In Westburn, who sets the bar higher? Chris will find it when he gets out of the Air Force, but you Nathan, must be near the Jazz ceiling of Westburn. It's that barrier; you need to get through it."

Mr. Monty took another swallow of Maker's Mark. "What they've done, Dorothy, is remarkable, but Westburn is a dead end. Where is the audience, the like-minded spirits? I like the town, and the people are douce, but it's in decline. Look around you. It won't die next year or the year after that, but in five or ten years?"

The worm of irritation was nipping at Nathan. "Chris, you'll be going home soon?" he said.

"End of November; enlistment's up then. But I'm not stayin' in Gary. Can't do what I want there, not anywhere in Indiana. I'm headin' for the West Coast."

"We'll miss you," Dorothy said.

"Well, I figure I'll miss you too," Chris said. "Come on over, Nathan. Let's play some out there."

Nathan looked at Dorothy. "I'm OK right now. It might be hard to find a job."

"You're a good welder," Chris said. "You'd find something. And you'd be at the heart of the music."

Dorothy turned away; Nathan touched her arm. "It's getting late, Dorothy. I'll walk you to your rooms."

They stood at the end of Galt Place, leaning on the retaining wall above the railway cutting, and gazed at the tracks sixty feet below.

"Were you mad at Mr. Monty?" Dorothy said.

"No no I'm not thick, Dorothy," Nathan said. "I hear what he's saying and I see Westburn as well as any man. But he did bang on a bit about why I should leave. Maybe there'll be a time when it's right to go, but not now. Ma isn't getting any younger. One of these days she might need me. And Mr. Monty, well, I'll look after him an' all if he needs it."

Dorothy rested her head on Nathan's shoulder. "Darling Nathan, oh, darling Nathan. I don't want you to go to North America."

Darling: not a word that Nathan used. It was used by posh Englishmen and easy going American actors, but Nathan was embarrassed when he heard it. But he felt good when Dorothy called him darling. "I like the way you said that."

"Said what?"

"You know."

"Tell me."

"Darling … darling, Dorothy."

Nathan would stay in Westburn because Dorothy wanted him to. Nathan couldn't imagine events unfolding that would change his mind. "I might have felt differently if we hadn't met, but now I want to stay with you."

Nathan was meeting Dorothy on the Sunday afternoon. Dressing, he was hot and randy. He left Galt Place early and took a long walk to Dorothy's rooms. His love and respect for Dorothy had held him in check, but when he got near her rooms he was dying for it. Nathan made a detour through quiet streets, and thought about a sweet time with a Japanese girl.

The Army sent Nathan on leave to Japan, and he was glad to get away from the fighting in Korea. He remembered little of Kure and even less of Japan, but he'd never forget the few days he spent with a sixteen-year old Pan-Pan girl. Her name was Betty. "Lrike a Betty Hutton," she said.

"Jesus, fuckin' Christ," Nathan said. How the Hell had this Jap kid fastened on to Betty Hutton? He saw her tears. "I'm so sorry. What's your Japanese name."

"Taeko. It means Beautiful Child."

Nathan was edgy, a couple of days out of Korea, but forgot that Taeko was sixteen and on the game. She was so petite and demure, smiling, looking up at his regimental Tam O' Shanter, flattering him when she picked him up. "I lrike Jocks," she said.

Taeko was a tart and she'd have preferred a GI with more money; if she'd been better looking Taeko would have had an American soldier. Instead, she had Nathan, a lanky Scot. Taeko was not hard and grasping, but she was firm about the cost of her services. Nathan was easy, and they soon agreed a price for the days he would stay with her. He was jangling after the fighting in Korea and Taeko the Pan-Pan girl, made him happy.

Nathan liked Taeko and felt good staying in her shabby rooms. She was so young and shy, taking her first steps in the profession. He loved the way she struggled to pronounce L and the smile on her moon face. Her hen-toed shuffle made him randy. When he lay with Taeko she made him feel wanted, and he felt close to her. He was thankful that a Japanese prostitute treated him with greater respect and fondness than any of his own kind.

The first time she was naked in front of him she pointed to her small breasts laughing shyly, covering her mouth to hide her shame.

"I like them," Nathan said. "They're lovely."

She touched the hair on his torso."Chinge." Taeko said.

And he touched the little mounds with the large brown nipples. He bent across her and kissed her left nipple and she smiled. Day after day she pleased Nathan. Taeko's fingers touched him and he did not resist. On the second morning, he got up and stretched out his stiffness and she smiled at his desire. Tenderly he held her head.

Taeko prepared him for making love and she guessed that it was Nathan's first time. She held him and he died inside her. "You touch my heart," Taeko said. And for those few days, he didn't feel lonely.

Nathan gave her money for food and drink. He was happy making love, giving in to her touch; to sleep, and forget the war. He paid her the day he left, then Nathan gave Taeko the money he had left. As the plane crossed the Sea of Japan, he felt he loved Taeko, but back at the front, he knew he hadn't.

At twenty-five, Nathan had resigned himself to life without women, finding emotional consolations in his music; then he'd met Dorothy and he was crazy about her.

They wandered through the quiet town. Ma was out visiting an old friend from her pawn broking days and would not return until well into the evening. They lingered in front of the Town Buildings, admiring the flowerbeds packed with marigolds, dahlias, and borders of yellow and purple pansies. A scattered flotilla of grey clouds drifted up the Firth, threatening broadsides of rain, casting shadows overhead. Dorothy held Nathan's hand, pressing and kneading his fingers, sending jolts to their very tips. Nathan returned the pressure, and she smiled at him.

"It's going to rain," Nathan said.

Few people were around when they turned into Provident Street. As he steered her into the corner, Nathan winced as their fingers laced tighter. He turned her, drawing her head under his chin. He loved the smell of her hair. "Let's go back to Galt Place. We'll be dry there."

Dorothy moved awkwardly around the silent kitchen, touching the kettle, and then wiping the already dried and cleaned dresser. Nathan liked the clicking of her heels on the lino. "I'll make tea," Nathan said.

"I don't want tea."

"Coffee?"

"No, not coffee."

Dorothy was lovely in her blue cotton summer dress with short sleeves. She removed her white kid gloves, tugging them finger by finger and laid them on the table next to her slim leather handbag.

Nathan moved round the table and stood next to her. "I like your gloves."

They embraced. His hand rested on her breast; a slow tender caress and he felt her nipple rise. "No, Nathan, not here."

Nathan drew the blind, and his bedroom was in shadow. He neatly folded his clothes, laying them on a chair. Dorothy had moved away from him into private space as she disrobed. Her shoes set to one side, and her clothes lay on the carpet. He watched her step out of her French knickers; a quick bending of one leg, then the other, and let them fall beside her dress and shoes. A shaft of sunlight lighted the ribbon of space between the edge of the blind and the window. Dorothy turned as the sun shone on her small pointed breasts and brown, crown-sized nipples. "Sweet Jesus," Nathan said, gazing at her long slender legs and hollow stomach, where fine hairs gathered in a glistering bush. He wondered what Dorothy thought of his hairy body.

Dorothy crossed her arms, hiding her breasts, and smiled nervously. She was just eighteen.

Nathan thought about stopping, but he could not. "Let me help." Nathan retrieved her clothes folding them on the top of a low chest of drawers. He tucked her shoes to one side. Impulsively, he put his arm round her shoulders and she looked at him. He ducked down, put his free arm behind her knees and lifted her up, took the few steps to his bed, and laid her down. Dorothy put her arm round his neck and kissed him.

He touched her, and she responded opening her legs a fraction. Dorothy was at the centre of Nathan's world, and he was tender. But it was awkward lovemaking and she yelped at the pain as he came near her. He caressed her again, and she touched him, and he fought the pleasures of her long fingers. He came near her again but stopped when she gasped in pain. They turned apart, backs touching. Nathan looked at the blood on his fingers.

Dorothy sat up. "I'm bleeding, I'm bleeding."

"I think it's my blood," Nathan said.

He returned from the bathroom with a wad of soft paper and handed it to her. She removed the drops of blood from the tops of her thighs.

"It was your blood. Oh, Nathan, I've hurt you. It's all my fault."

"No, no. I was too quick."

Nathan got rid of the paper. He came back and crept in beside her. They were both gloomy and humble: believing that they had failed and had fallen from a high place. Dorothy lay against him in shallow sleep. He blamed himself, but it was no one's fault. Dorothy was young and frightened, and he was too eager.

The rain drummed on the window, and Nathan looked at his watch. Four o'clock and they'd been drifting in and out of sleep for almost an hour, too embarrassed to say anything. He knew that he must try again with Dorothy.

Nathan rolled over to Dorothy and put his arm round her shoulder. He wanted to show how much he loved her. "Dorothy, are you all right?" She turned and he saw the streaks of dried tears on her cheeks. Nathan reached for his handkerchief. "Put your tongue out." He dabbed a corner of the handkerchief on the tip of her tongue. Then wiped away her tears. "That's better, isn't it?"

"Yes."

"I never meant to hurt you. I'm sorry."

"I'm sorry I cried so."

Nathan decided to tell her. "I love you very much. This has been the best summer of my life."

"I know, Nathan. And I love you."

They were in a better place. "We can make love. Don't be afraid."

"All right."

He uncovered Dorothy and laid a pillow beside her. "Lie on the pillow." Nathan touched her in all the sweet places and Dorothy was glad. And Nathan was happy when she reached for him. "Hold me," he said.

Nathan imagined Dorothy pregnant and himself killed down the yard. Then Dorothy would be alone. Who would care for her if he lay dead on the hull of the submarine? Horse Jones would send Dorothy away to have the child, or worse, to abort, and Nathan's soul would not rest.

But for now they were glad to have found a way to love. So they went to Nathan's room when Ma was out and were happy.

Chapter Four

They heard a guitarist and a horn player improvise. "That's Crazy She Calls Me," Nathan said.

"I know," Dorothy said, standing close to him. smiling. "You played the piano and sang it to me when I was convalescing."

Dorothy was happy after the troubles with Zoë. Her fair hair was full and shining, skin clear and smooth, the scar on her brow was fading, and her eyes flashed with joy when she was with Nathan. She was in her glory, slender and feminine.

People gathered, drawn by the guitar and flugel horn exploring the song, teasing out its mysteries. The beauty of the song captured in the restrained, soulful mood, an intuitive conversation between the players and shared with anyone that wanted to listen. The musicians handed the lead back and forth; the guitarist, improvising, exploring the bluesy melancholy suggestions of the flugel horn, then shifting to chords and sounding of drums and voices as the flugel horn coaxed the guitarist to a dazzling finish.

The song drew Dorothy closer to Nathan, and she sang, a sweet, fragile voice so that only Nathan heard.

"I say I'll move the mountains
And I'll move the mountains
If he wants them out of the way

Crazy he calls me
Sure, I'm crazy
Crazy in love, I say."

"Jesus, Dorothy," Nathan said, and bent to kiss her hair.

"You're a swell singer, Kid," Chris said.

"Oh, Chris," Dorothy said, blushing deeply.

"They can play," Nathan said. "Jazz on a Summer Day."

"What a sound," Leo said. "An' that flugel horn. Ye need to get one, Nathan. Man, we could make new music."

"Oh, go on, Nathan," Dorothy said. "It would be wonderful."

Nathan smiled. "I'll see if I can scare up the money."

The band was ready. It was a great honour to be invited; and to be paid: the band would have played free just to be there. Nathan was glad that Leo drove the band hard at rehearsals and that Dorothy was there to listen to his worries about the arrangements.

Nathan stretched, seeking cool air to escape the warm, heavy atmosphere. The sight of a drunken Philomena wandering through the crowd troubled him. God knows what she might do if she kept on drinking. He turned west and gazed at the cloud formations hanging above Westburn. The coming shift in the weather made him uneasy.

Nathan saw Philomena again later in the afternoon. In happier times she might have been performing; that day she was a spectator. Leo had been right about her drinking. She looked rough: blotchy complexion, a patchwork quilt of red hues, coarse skin, eyelids weighted by dark pouches.

People danced when Chris sang the Louis Jordan song; 'I Want You To Be My Baby.' Nathan left the stage for the last part of the song and danced with Dorothy laughingly whispering the lyrics to her.

"I,
I want, I want,
I want you,
I want you to be
I want you to be my baby.
Will,
Will you, will you please,
Will you please tell me,
If you're going to be my baby."

The audience swayed to Chris' singing. Nathan and Dorothy slowly turned in their private circle. Nathan's voice and Dorothy's humming of the tune, and they knew that they loved one another. "Dorothy, Dorothy," Nathan said holding her close. "I know, Nathan, I know," Dorothy said.

The sky darkened, and the sunset turned the edges of the Cumulonimbus a deep red. The evening air heavy and damp; the oppressive heat promised rain as they finished stowing the drums and bass on the bus, back to Westburn. Nathan, Leo, and Chris took their instruments on the bus.

The American guitarist and the flugel horn player walked over. "We like what you played. Great version of Now's The Time," the horn player said.

"Thanks," Nathan said. To be recognized by these professionals pleased Nathan.

"Any of you ever played across the pond?" the guitarist said.

"I have," Chris said. "I'm going home soon; my enlistment in the Air Force is up. I'm heading for San Francisco."

"Ah played in the dance band of the Queen Mary on the Southampton-New York run for a while," Leo said. "Ah met an alto player in Charlie's Tavern. Ah sat in a few times."

"On 7th Avenue at 52nd and 53rd?" the horn player said. "I go there myself. A great place. What about you?"

"No," Nathan said. "Just here."

"You should get over there; stretch yourself some," the guitarist said. He got his wallet out and removed some cards, handing them round. "We're living in Vancouver now. Nice town; good Jazz scene. If you ever get over look us up. Maybe we can work something out."

A distant flash of sheet lightning lit the cloud, muffled thunder overhead. Heavy drops of warm rain spattered the ground ricocheting off the dust. A steady downpour, turning dust to a syrupy mud.

"The summer day's ending," Nathan said. His arm around Dorothy's shoulder and he felt damp spots on her dress. She pressed closer. The warm rain fell on them, and the group broke apart, moving onto the bus, the Americans running towards the car park.

Nathan did not see Philomena get on the bus. She'd travelled to the Festival by another vehicle. There was no escaping her, when twenty minutes from Westburn, she shot out of her seat, lurching along the passageway of the speeding vehicle. She barely kept her footing as she stood over them, exhaling fumes of stale smoke, whisky and beer.

"So this is the burd?" Philomena said, jerking her head at Dorothy.

"You'd better sit down, before you fall down," Nathan said. "Go back to your seat."

"Who the fuck 'ye talkin' tae, ya bastard?"

Heads turned. Dorothy looked from Nathan to Philomena and back to Nathan. He felt sick.

"So you're the wee fuckin' swank?" Philomena said. "Ye look a right cunt."

Nathan got out of his seat, shaking off Dorothy's hand. Far away he heard the rumble of tyres on the road and the crunch of gears as the driver slowed down. He considered throttling

Philomena, and took hold of her shoulder. "Come on, Philo. I'll take you back to your seat."

Philomena held on to the back of a seat. "Get yer fuckin' hans aff me, ya fuckin' bastard."

Nathan glanced at Dorothy, and she stared at him. Philomena leaned across the back of the seat, her rank breath enveloping Dorothy. "Didnae tell ye aboot me, did he? The fuckin' shite. A' wan time yer precious Nathan could nae get enough o' me. He wis humpin' me regular."

People stared, and far away Nathan heard Philomena shrieking at Dorothy. "He wis fuckin' shaggin' me. Aye, an' that's jist the half o' it. Liked it dirty; stickin' it up ma arse."

Philomena reached into a bag hanging from her shoulder. There was a plop as she pulled the cork from a near empty half bottle of whisky and slurped down a long swig. Whisky ran down the corners of her mouth.

Nathan had enough. "Go back to your seat. You're a disgrace."

"Fuck off. You'll no' tell me whit tae dae."

Philomena emptied the half bottle. Nathan pushed her back, as the vomit shot out of her mouth onto the front of her dress. Philomena retched loudly and sent puke over Nathan's shirt. He heard Dorothy crying, "Oh, oh." "Surely it can't get any worse," he muttered. The bus stopped a couple of hundred yards from Westburn Police Station.

The driver was beside them, and grabbed Philomena's shoulder "Right, you. Off now or it's the Police. An' you two an' all," he said.

"Let the girl stay," Nathan said.

"Ah said off now, Mate. The fuckin' lot of you."

Dorothy ignored Nathan's hand and squeezed past. The bus was quiet. Dorothy, Nathan, Philomena, and the bus driver crowded the narrow passageway. Philomena laughed. A blast of her wind followed by whoosh and gurgle as her bowels emptied. The bus stank and a man sniggered.

Nathan, stuck a forefinger in his face. "Wipe the smile off yer face, Mate."

"That's it,"the driver said. "Ah'm gettin' the Police right now."

Nathan caught the driver by his tie, tightening it. The driver struggled for breath. Nathan punched him in the stomach and held him up. "Go near the police an' Ah'll come fur ye; an' Ah'll find ye."

Nathan wanted Dorothy away from this horror to protect her from a night in the cells among drunks and brawlers, and the scandal of a charge of Breach of the Peace in the Police Court. Nathan, the Westburn hardman, was ashamed.

They got off the bus into the rain, and the bus pulled away from the kerb. Philomena passed out and slumped into the rainwater bubbling on the pavement. She stank horribly. Nathan looked at the puke and shit staining his clothes.

Philomena's filth marked Dorothy's white summer dress. She backed away from Nathan, splashing through a filthy puddle that rose around her slim ankles, her hands out rejecting him. "No, no," she said, turned and walked away from him towards Valentia and her own people.

"What a waste," Nathan said. Philomena curled up on the wet pavement in a drunken stupor. He remembered how well she used to sing and the good days when he played with her, but she'd wasted her talent. He regretted that she'd squandered her gifts and turned to leave, but could not. He could not desert her to be picked up by the police, dumped in the cells charged with being drunk and incapable.

Philomena's tenement flat was nearby so Nathan prodded her awake and half-carried her home. He staggered off and on pavements and forgot about his disgusting appearance, but he worried about Dorothy. He wanted to speak to her, hold her, and make things right.

"Ah'm goin' tae ma bed," Philomena said. "Sleep it aff."

"No. Drink this." Nathan made her finish the glass of salted water. She vomited, emptying her stomach. "Fuck you, Nathan Forrest. Ye should've let me sleep."

"You stink," Nathan said. "Get undressed and into the bath."

Nathan waited in the living room, knocking the bathroom door from time to time, looking in to see that she'd not passed out, slipping down and drowning in her grey bathwater.

Nathan worried again about Dorothy. Surely it couldn't be over between them? He must see Dorothy soon and make it right, but he was angry at Dorothy's abrupt departure. Nathan was anxious that they'd not make it up.

He turned down Philomena's bed revealing grubby sheets, and switched on the bed light. Nathan looked around the bedroom; it had grown shabbier since he'd last been there: cigarette burns on the carpet by the side of the bed and on the counterpane. A sure sign that Philomena was smoking in bed, falling asleep, a lighted cigarette dropping from her fingers.

She might pass out again, set the bedding alight, burning herself to death. He put on the main light. Philomena appeared in the bedroom doorway, a towel wound round her damp hair, a shabby robe tied at the waist. Her haggard face was shrouded in the smoke of a cigarette hanging from her lips.

"Lay aff the smoking tonight," Nathan said, pointing to the burns, plucking the cigarette from her mouth, and extinguishing it. Her breath reeked of stale whisky.

"Aye, aye, OK, OK," Philomena said, staggering as she approached the bed.

Philomena threw her robe across the bottom of the bed. Her night dress was grubby. She swung her legs up. He saw the dirt half-moons on her toenails. A smile split her raddled face. "Ye fancy a bit?"

"Good night," Nathan said, closing the bedroom door behind him, and letting himself out of the flat.

It was after two when Nathan got home. Ma, who usually stayed awake until he came in, had fallen into a sound sleep. He wrapped his soiled clothing in a parcel, then slowly ran a bath not to waken Ma. He bathed.

Nathan rose at six in the morning and dressed quietly. He ate an apple and headed for the yard and his half shift of Sunday overtime.

"OK, Mate?" he said to the riveter, standing by the glowing brazier heating rivets, and threw the parcel of his clothing into the flames. His soiled clothing vanished in the heat of pale yellow coals.

Nathan had not slept well; was not concentrating on the job and had a dressing down for a botched weld by a badly hung over foreman. When he left the yard, he was wretched and stopped at a phone box to call Dorothy. The old lady Cooke said, "She isn't at home." He tried again at the dinner break on the Monday, but Dorothy was not at home to him.

Monday evening, two days since the Jazz Festival on Saturday when Nathan thought life was good. Leo came. They had not met down the yard, and he knew that Nathan would want to talk. And he brought the Bach that Nathan had left on the bus.

"Thanks, Leo," Nathan said.

"Ye OK, Nathan; any word from Dorothy?"

"Nothing. I called her twice and she wouldn't come to the phone. Got to tell you Leo, I'm fuckin' pissed at Dorothy for that."

"Nathan, for Christ's sake. Don't talk like that. Dorothy's a nice girl. Don't say things you'll regret. Philomena's the bad news; no' Dorothy."

Ma called from her bedroom. "Nathan. Bring me in the paper." Lately, Ma had taken to having 'wee rests' in the late afternoon and early evening, feeling worn out. But, when Nathan urged her to see the doctor, she'd brushed his concerns aside. "Ah'll be fine a couple of weeks."

Nathan took the unopened evening paper to Ma. "Are ye goin' tae tell Ma the whole story?" Leo said.

"Ma thinks the world of Dorothy. She knows we've fallen out and she's upset."

"Nathan, Leo." Ma called. "Come here, quick."

Ma handed them The Westburn Gazette. On the bottom half of the front page there was a photograph of a younger, prettier Philomena under the headline: Local Singer Found Dead. A neighbour discovered the body.

"Drinking," Leo said. "Fell asleep, drowned in her own puke."

There was a resume of her career and the journalist made the cheap shot that Philomena had struggled unsuccessfully with drink. Philomena left no estate and there were no living relatives. The Local Authority would attend to her funeral arrangements.

"That's a pauper's funeral," Ma said. "Damn her for hurtin' Dorothy, but a pauper's funeral. That's no' right."

So, Ma raided her Gurdy. Nathan got it from the gig money kept in his drawer. "The wife's the treasurer," Leo said. "Ah'll get cash from her." They'd give Philomena a decent funeral. Nathan and Leo made the arrangements.

"Ah hope this blues sounds a'right," Nathan said.

"It'll sound fine," Leo said. "Don't worry."

Nathan sat in front with Leo. Chuck and Joe were in the back of the battered Humber estate, following the hearse carrying Philomena's remains. The cortege slowly navigated Westburn's streets, old men stopped and removed their caps; women stood until they passed and made the Sign of the Cross. In 1958, there was still respect for the dead.

Nathan worried about Ma. That morning Ma, clutching her painful stomach, went back to her bed. Nathan called the doctor for a house visit in the afternoon.

The vast cemetery swept by a strong north west breeze bending trees, scattering flower petals, leaves from wreaths and plants adorning graves. Grey skies over the open grave. There was no bird song. A winter's day in September, and they waited for the undertaker's men to bring the coffin.

A few yards away the gravediggers, black silhouettes leaning on long-shafted shovels. Back from the grave a handful of musicians and admirers of Philomena waited. The quality had not come. No lawyers, doctors, or accountants; the people to whom she'd given pleasure in her heyday; or the few who'd shared her bed when she was girlish and pretty.

"Fuckin' Westburn," Nathan said.

Philomena would have laughed at a man in a dog collar who knew nothing about her, stumbling through a hasty eulogy. The band did what it could, sending Philomena across to the other side with a song. They shuffled awkwardly by the graveside. Then they were still. Nathan fingered the Bach's valves and Leo slung his alto. Joe put the snare drum on its stand, the feet sinking into the damp earth. Chuck cradled the Bass, its point resting on a flat stone.

They played St Louis Blues inspired by Armstrong, Longshaw and Bessie Smith. The wind fractured the music, sending it to the far corners of the cemetery. Rose blooms snapped off stems and littered the ground. Leaves tore from trees, and Dahlia petals flying, all swirling in the air, and falling down.

"Gentleman," the undertaker said, and they took four cords of the coffin. The undertaker's men and one of the gravediggers took up the remaining four cords. "Together, now," he said. And they lowered the polished oak coffin into the grave.

"Amen," Nathan said, when the coffin hit bottom. They let go the cords, a ragged clatter as soft, braided rope struck oak.

Nathan looked at the heap of damp earth that the gravediggers would shovel into the lair. The untidiness of a new grave would vanish, and it would look better when the small headstone was erected: Philomena O'Donnell (June Connor) Jazz Singer 1920-1958 RIP.

Leo parked the Humber near his tenement flat, and they removed the instruments to his apartment. They walked down Michael Street prominent in dark suits, white shirts, and the black ties of mourners, their steel heel tips ringing off the granite pavement.

An old man stopped them. "Too bad aboot Philomena. She wisnae a bad singer." He shook hands with all four.

In the Long Known Bar, Eddie the barman placed halfs of whisky and half pint beer chasers in front of them. "Ye'll need a wee livener, boys."

The others sipped whisky and beer. Nathan turned the whisky glass round in his hand; the gantry lights shimmering in the golden spirit. He inhaled the aroma of the whisky; a wounding swallow, the hoppy beer chaser; and several more until the pain of losing Dorothy was gone. He put the glass down. "Thanks, Eddie, but Ah'll pass."

"That's a' right, Nathan."

At table they juggled hot shell pies, taking small bites, chewing gingerly and sucking air to cool the hot mince and pastry before they swallowed.

"We've somethin' tae tell ye," Chuck said. Chuck and Joe had found jobs in the band of the P&O liner Orsova on the Southampton-Australia run. They were leaving next week missing the next gig.

"Sorry tae tell ye this the day," Joe said. "We came on a lot playin' you and Chris."

"We've had enough o' drillin' doon the yerd," Chuck said.

"If Ah never see it again, it'll be too soon," Joe said.

"It's the right thing," Nathan said. "Good luck," Leo said. It was the finish of the band, and a dead end when Chris left.

Eddie came over and handed them the early edition of the Westburn Gazette. "Inside, the middle pages."

There was a respectful note. A dignified ceremony and a few friends had laid Philomena to rest. "That reporter did the decent thing," Leo said.

Nathan shrugged; with the funeral over, all he could think about was Dorothy.

"Come on, Nathan," Leo said. "Let's get up the road and see Ma."

Two weeks later Dorothy posted back the Cashmere shawl. There was no letter. It upset Ma. Nathan drew the fine wool of the shawl against his face, searching for a trace of Dorothy's cologne. He refolded the shawl, and placed it in his drawer. Then rage came. He wanted to lash out at Dorothy, considered sending back the records she'd given him, but he was above such a cheap shot.

Nathan grew angrier at Dorothy's refusal to speak to him. He took a day off work to have it out with her. Nathan waited in the shadow of the Town Kirk, near her rooms.

She came down the steps from the Cookes' house, so pretty in a short wool coat, the scissoring of her slender legs and the sound of her footsteps cut now that she'd gone. He loved her. "Hello, Dorothy," Nathan said, stepping from the shadow of the Kirk, standing in front of her the shawl in a parcel under his arm. Dorothy paused mid stride and veered to pass. Nathan blocked her way.

"You're not going to walk by me?"

"What do you want?" she said, her face a distant grown up mask.

"I'd like you to have the shawl. I gave it to you; it belongs to you. Can't we talk things over; go for a walk, have a coffee somewhere?"

Nathan was ashamed, pleading. They stood on the pavement, the silence lasted about fifteen seconds; for Nathan it could have been fifteen years.

"I don't want the shawl, or anything of yours."

"It was bad, what happened. You don't think that I had anything to do with it?"

"You went out with that dreadful slut; you were her lover. Just let me pass."

A teacher from the nearby Academy Grammar, wearing an academic gown stopped. "I say Miss, are you all right?" He was about Nathan's build. Nathan hated his superior West End drawl. Nathan's work-toughened hand caught the academic gown, bunching it into a rough knot at the shoulder, jerking his head back. "Mind yer own business, Mate."

The teacher's face turned grey, and he wilted under Nathan's hard look. He hurried away, the academic gown flapping behind him.

"You were going to hit that man," Dorothy said. "Just as you hit the bus driver."

"Aye, an' so what? You haven't a clue. We were heading for the cells that night. That driver was a clown, a nasty piece of work. Ah had to stop him going to the police."

"I suppose you're back with that woman."

Nathan, hand on Dorothy's shoulder. "Dorothy, Dorothy, it's all right; don't be jealous. I told you I'd known an older woman. I'd given her up and quit drinking. I haven't seen her in three years." Nathan had to make it right. "I love you," he said.

Dorothy stared straight ahead. "You sodomized her. That's what you wanted to do to me. Is that what bastard Catholics do; bugger their women?"

Nathan eyes filled with tears and hate. "Ah never thought you'd say that to me. You're just like all the rest of them, you and your kind. Ah don't remember you shying away from me. You liked the taste of me well enough when you came to ma bedroom."

He stepped aside to let her pass. "Goodbye, Nathan."

"Philomena's deid. Leo an' me buried her last week."

"I'm sorry."

"Sorry? Whit're ye sorry for? She wis jist a fuckin' slut. Philomena hud talent an' she could sing an' she wasted it. She understood music better than a' they fuckin' pratts at the Athenaeum. Philo never had a fuckin' chance; workin' in a tin box factory. Her fuckin' right hand wis mangled in a machine when she wis eighteen. People fae this side," he gestured towards the West End, "like yer Old Man, used her. Ah knew her well, an' Ah never heard that her faither beat her up or her fuckin' auntie put her in the infirmary."

Nathan saw the grown up mask vanish and Dorothy was the girl he loved. "I hate you, Nathan Forrest," she said.

Nathan stuck a finger in her face. "Never darken my fuckin' door."

He tightened his arm on the Cashmere shawl, her sobbing following him as he headed for Galt Place and his own people.

Chapter Five

An anxious Nathan stood by the infirmary bed. Ma had lain there for two weeks, resting between tests, and examinations. Ma had wasted away, face damp, shallow hurried breathing. Turning, he gazed out the tall window to the old cemetery with its flat gravestones, untidy turf and gravel paths. He went there with Dorothy to see the grave of the novelist, John Galt.

A hand touched his arm. "Mr. Forrest? I'm Hamilton, Consultant in charge of Mrs. Forrest. Would you come over to the Ward Office? I'd like a word."

The cup of tea grew cold in Nathan's hand; what Hamilton said stunned him. Ma had a tumor in her stomach. He would operate the next day and remove what he could of the tumor. There would be a period of remission; perhaps several weeks. Ma had three months at most to live.

"Mrs. Forrest will be quite bright for a time when you get her home," Hamilton said. "Then her decline will be rapid and she'll come back to the Infirmary where we can provide the care she'll need."

"For Christ's sake. Her name's Ma. I'll take care of her."

"All right, Mr. Forrest, I'll call her Ma," Hamilton said pouring hot tea into Nathan's cup. "Your intentions are commendable, but frankly, they are not practical. The end won't be pleasant.

And what about your job? Ma will need constant care. I urge you to reconsider."

"I said, I'll take care of her. I'll get leave of absence from the yard," Nathan said, slapping the desk.

"Mr. Forrest, please calm down."

"I'm sorry, Mr. Hamilton. I know you're trying to do what's best for Ma. But she'd rather be at home."

"Very well. We'll help, of course, and the District Nurse will come in every day."

Horse Jones, back from Istanbul filled with praise from the Turkish Navy denied Nathan's request for leave of absence. The Welfare Officer and the Shop Steward told him what happened. "This is a shipyard," Jones said. "We do Naval work. He can put her in hospital where she belongs. Forrest can stay or go. If he leaves, there's no guarantee he'll get his job back."

The Shop Steward said that forcing Nathan, a good tradesman, to hand in his notice would not be popular with the men. "Don't threaten me," Jones said. "I don't give a fuck about the men or about Forrest. But I do give a fuck about building submarines."

They rejected Nathan's claim for unemployment benefit; he'd quit his job. The clerk suggested he seek benefit from the National Assistance Board. "We'll have nuthin' tae dae wi' them," Ma said. "Nuthin' but meddlers and busy bodies nosin' into our business. We'll manage fine, son."

Before he quit, the men had a whip and collected a generous sum, enough to cover living expenses for four or five weeks. "That's very kind," Ma said. Ma controlled the household cash with her Gurdy. Mr. Monty looked after her savings; she'd call on him when money was short.

Nathan was unemployed when the priest came to the house, hearing that Ma was very ill. "I'm Father Toner. I want to see Mrs. Forrest," he said. Nathan kept him at the door.

"I know who you are," Nathan said. Toner, School Chaplain, and Parish hearty, kept youth on the right path; of the tribe that would have taken Nathan from his grandparents. Once, Toner mentioned Nathan's illegitimacy in front of the class; then he beat him. Nathan detested his pose of gruff genial Irishman. He let Toner squeeze through the door. "You've got five minutes."

Toner got to work. "Nathan's doin' a grand job, and God will reward him. But Millie, listen to me. Ye'd be better looked after in the Little Sisters' Home. Sure they have everything necessary to take care of ye."

The Little Sisters of The Poor were good and kind but determined to save souls. They'd pester Ma to pray and confess her sins. The nuns would terrify Ma. She would be in the arms of death in the last days of her life. Nathan wanted Ma in the embrace of life until her time came.

"Ah'm fine here, Father."

Toner bored on, "Leave us now, Nathan, and I'll hear Millie's confession. I'll give ye the Blessed Sacrament. Sure ye want to make a good Confession and come back to the Church and God's love."

"Ma's staying here. Leave her be."

Toner turned his back on Nathan. "Ye want to confess, Millicent; ye know ye do. Embrace God's Mercy and He'll give ye absolution."

Ma shook her head and turned into her pillow. Nathan would not have objected had Ma wanted to confess and return to the Faith.

"Who'll take care of ye at the end?" Toner said.

"Mr. Monty. He'll be taking care of my funeral; him and Nathan."

Toner scowled, "And who might he be?"

"Montague Solomon," Ma said. "A good man, a kind man."

"He's a good friend," Nathan said.

"Solomon." Toner said. "A Jew; it won't do. In God's name: a Jew. It won't do at all."

"Listen, Mister," Nathan said, "If they piled up all the priests in Westburn and ye stood on the top of them, you'd not be big enough to kiss Mr. Monty's arse."

Ma drifted into a shallow sleep. Toner squared up to Nathan, thinking of the youthful boxer he'd once been.

"Leave," Nathan said. "Yer frightening Ma." Toner was afraid of Nathan's eyes: the hurt at Ma's approaching death; a black fury that he could not pin down. And Toner was scared, but hid it behind a snort of disgust as he left.

All the days were not grim, and in the intervals when Ma was free from pain, Nathan sat with her and they were consoled by views of the mountains across the river in the clear autumn light. On these days, after he'd got her into a comfortable chair, put on her slippers, and wrapped a blanket round her legs, Ma had Nathan fetch the photographs.

Ma stared a long time at the photograph of Nathan, a serious mite in his Christening robes, the fine white Cashmere shawl draped around his shoulders, the long tassels arranged at his hips snaking out on the surface of the photographer's table, his tiny feet poking out from the hem of the robe. Looking at the photograph, seeing the shawl again, the shawl that Dorothy had accepted so affectionately, brought back to Nathan her cruel words and his coarse response, when he gave into the siren call of rage as she rejected his attempt at reconciliation.

Dorothy had been vindictive, but that was poor consolation for his own destructive actions. In those few minutes his goading and savagery had put Dorothy beyond reach, destroying any lingering affection she might have had for him.

Ma put the picture down and asked Nathan to pass her another favourite. She had always liked the picture of twelve-year-old Nathan in outsize bandsman's cap, clutching a cornet, staring out from the stiff ranks of the Catholic men in St Michael's Silver Band; and the studio portrait of Nathan, kilted in the uniform of Highland Infantry.

"Yer Grandfather was a fine man," Ma said, pointing to a black and white photograph of Nathan, James and herself taken on a day trip to the seaside just before the War.

Nathan had put away the studio portrait of Dorothy and himself, but Ma kept her copy in a silver frame on the dressing table: and she often gazed at it. Then, Nathan had to look, and he felt bittersweet anguish, staring at the sepia print taken with a 19th Century camera. Dorothy refined, the hem of her dress covering her knees. He saw that she was in love with him: the photographer had caught the moment. Nathan's hand rested confidently on Dorothy's shoulder. When he looked at her photograph he heard her words; a ghastly, rhythmic mantra that made him feel sick, "You sodomized her. Is that what Catholic bastards do; bugger their women? That's what you wanted to do to me."

Nathan withdrew into reverie, remembering his delight when Dorothy told him about the appointment at the studio on a Saturday morning before he went to Glasgow for the class. He'd waited for her in the Cookes' sitting room. Nathan had dressed carefully to please Dorothy.

"You're very smart, Nathan," she said as she came into the sitting room.

"You're not so bad yourself, Dorothy," he said as he kissed her.

"Nathan, you'll crush my dress."

He held her at arm's length, admiring the blue cotton dress that he'd asked her to wear, and the slim black leather handbag she carried. Dorothy seemed taller, a young lady, and he glanced down at her new high-heeled shoes.

"Jesus, Dorothy, you look great," he said, his love for her breaking through his gruffness.

"All gone," Nathan said.

Nathan became an adept at turning Ma in bed to relieve stiffness and prevent bedsores. Then he'd anoint her heels, her hips, and her elbows with zinc ointment. He used tender hands to lift Ma on to the bedpan and when she was strong enough eased her from her bed on to the commode that the Infirmary had supplied. He bathed her modestly, and the District Nurse attended to her intimate toilet. But sometimes, Nathan dealt with incontinence, bed baths, and the regular changing of sheets. He cut her toenails and manicured her hands.

Nathan bought a washing machine, the first in Galt Place. He washed and wrung out bedclothes, drying them on racks that he'd set up by the fire in the kitchen and in the sitting room. With loving care he ironed the sheets and took special pride with Ma's nightdresses and bed jackets, finishing them to a fine smoothness. The house in Galt Place was devoted to Ma's welfare. Neighbours came bringing food and taking washing away from Nathan, sitting with Ma to let him take a short walk.

Chris came a day or two before flying home. Nathan went to the kitchen to make tea.

"How you doin', Ma?" Chris said as he sat by her bedside.

"Ach Ah'm done, son. It's time Ah wis away."

"Come on, Ma. Don't give up. We'd be lost without you."

"Ah'll try Chris, but Ah'm so damned tired. Yer a good boy, Chris, comin' to see me."

From the kitchen, they heard the kettle boiling and the rattle of teaspoons on cups and saucers. Nathan would be back in a minute or two when the tea had infused. Ma struggled to get upright and Chris put his arm under her shoulders, bringing her up. She was skin and bone.

"What is it, Ma?"

"Help me, Chris. Ah worry about Nathan and what'll happen to him when Ah'm gone. Get him away from Westburn. There's nuthin' here for him. Oh, if he only had Dorothy."

"I'll try, Ma. I'll see what I can do."

Chris doubted that Nathan would pay heed to him.

They were quiet, drinking tea. Chris and Nathan nibbled at tea biscuits.

"Tell Chris about Mr.Youngman," Ma said.

"Ach, well, it was a bit embarrassing."

Leo or his wife came to sit with Ma on a Saturday and let Nathan attend his class in the Athenaeum and the afternoon lesson with Thomas Youngman. After several weeks out of work, money was short.

"Stop? Stop coming, Mr. Forrest? No, no, we can't have that. Your fees are paid at the Athenaeum for this term. You must continue and get your certificate. Don't worry about next term. There's the student welfare fund and I'll see to it, if it's necessary. Forget about my fee for now," Thomas Youngman said, as he turned away to sort through a folio of sheet music.

"Thank you, Mr.Youngman," Nathan said a deep blush on his face and neck.

"Hey, that's good, Nathan," Chris said.

The moments of silence extended; words failed to come and it was time for Chris to leave. "I have to go. When I get discharged from the Air Force, I'll head home to see Mom. Jeez Gary, Indiana. Then I'm going to San Francisco."

Chris had dreaded this farewell. Until he was posted to Scotland, he'd never been inside a white man's house. Nathan and Leo had brought him home soon after they met and it was plain that they respected him as a man and a musician; invited him to play with the band. He spent weekend passes staying with them. Ma treated him like a lost son far from home.

"Ma, you look after yourself, OK? I'll be seeing you."

Ma nodded, smiling, and raised her hand in farewell, too tired to speak.

"You be OK for ten minutes while Ah walk Chris to the station?" Nathan said.

Ma nodded and waved them away as she turned her head to her pillow and fell into a shallow sleep.

They crossed Provident Street to walk through the Well Park and down the steps to the back door of the Central Station. A November day and the park was empty, save for a few solitary old men and women walking a dog or hurrying home to the warmth of the fireside. The autumn wind tugged at the solitary leaves hanging on the oaks and the plane trees. Dead leaves gusted round Nathan and Chris' legs and fell into loose heaps as the west wind failed.

"Ah brought Dorothy here in June; first time we went out together."

"You ever hear anything from her? No chance of getting back with her?"

"No. Ah guess she's in St Andrew's at the University."

Nathan stopped at the Old Well. Dorothy had admired it, and the memory of her standing there, girlish and lovely in her red summer dress with the white fleur de lis motif, holding her white sun hat against her leg, squinting up at him through sunlight struck a blow and the pain in Nathan's stomach returned.

"Ah went to see her. She wouldn't answer the phone so Ah stopped her in the street. We had a terrible row. That finished it. Jesus Christ, Chris, she's eighteen and Ah'm tied in knots over her."

"I'm sorry for both of you. She always seemed like a nice kid. I liked her. You have to get out of here, Nathan, when Ma's gone. Cross the pond. Try the US; go to Canada."

"Ah can't think that far ahead. One thing: whatever happens, Ah'm not going down the yard again. The man that forced me out; that was Horse Jones, Dorothy's father. No one's going to treat me like shit ever again."

"Dorothy would have nothing to do with that."

Nathan shrugged. "Well, maybe, and maybe she's just like her fuckin' Old Man."

Chris drew him a strange look and shook his head. "Ah'm sorry I said that, Chris. Ah don't really think she'd do that to me."

Clouds of tart smelling white steam billowed out of the tunnel and the train pulled into the platform. They shook hands, but it wasn't enough for Chris. "You're like my brother, man," Chris said as he embraced Nathan.

"Look after yourself, Chris. Good luck in San Francisco. Ah'll be seeing you."

"Make it over there," Chris said as he opened the door and stepped up and into the carriage.

As the train moved off, its wheels slipping on the rails then gripping as it gained momentum, Chris released the leather strap securing the carriage window and leant out to wave.

Nathan stopped, turned, and raised his hand. Then he was gone through the main door of the station and back into Westburn.

Chapter Six

Nathan knew that Ma was declining, when one morning, the District Nurse removed her shoes and straddled Ma so that she might be turned in her bed with the minimum of pain. He too became adept at turning Ma as she retreated from life, decreasing her pain, and following the Nurse's advice, crossing Ma's legs at the ankles, turning her easily by holding her feet.

The appetite of the tumour was voracious, and Ma suffered agonies, relieved only when the Nurse gave an injection knocking her unconscious. At the Infirmary, a physician searched to find the combination of opiates to relieve her pain and leave her wakened. He worked intensely for a day until he broke through.

The District Nurse came in twice a day to administer blessed relief and wakefulness; and sometimes at night, stunning the cancer for a few hours knocking Ma out for sleep.

In these days of Ma's decline, Nathan forgot about Jazz, and his pain at losing Dorothy withered. Paying greater attention to Ma's grooming, doing everything possible to maintain her morale transported him from the inevitability of Ma's death. Ma, weakening daily from the cancer, was letting go, but she liked when the District Nurse arranged her hair an for a time, cheered her up making her feel part of life. Ma's grooming was more important for Nathan than simply keeping her cheerful: attending to her comfort, taking care of her feet and hands, frequently anointing heels, and elbows, shoulders, and hips; those parts of her wasting body that would be troubled by bed sores, had he not applied the Zinc and Castor Oil Ointment; the comforting routine of these tasks and Nathan's quiet tenderness, let Ma know that he loved her.

More difficult to manage were the days he helped the Nurse to bathe Ma: encouraged by the nurse, sometimes he sponged her wasted flesh as the Nurse supported and gently turned her; at other times, he supported and moved Ma, averting his eyes as the Nurse made good Ma's personal toilet.

Ma was too weak to leave her bed for the WC; nor had she the strength to get up and move a few feet to the commode. Nathan was at his most discreet and gentle as he turned Ma on her side and rolled her onto the bed pan. Ma's embarrassment, when he came back to the bedroom to clean her and to empty the bed pan, vexed him deeply; one day he felt that he could not go on, and lingered in the bathroom until he recovered, flushing the WC several times to hide his tears.

There were few cheerful days now as the cancer attacks grew and Ma gave ground to death. One bright day in that black winter, close to the end, Nathan moved her bed near the window, hurt, as she gasped at the pain as he propped her up; and he sat with her so that Ma looked over chimney tops and across the river to the high hills and mountains on the other side.

"Ah love this view, Nathan."

"It's nice, right enough."

"Ah'm very tired, son."

"Ah know, Ma."

"Ah'm so sorry about Dorothy. Ah would like to have seen her."

"Aye, well."

Ma roused herself and for a moment her voice was strong. "You get away from here, Nathan; leave Westburn. You listen to Mr. Monty, son."

"OK Ma; so Ah will."

Nathan could no longer evade the certainty of Ma's demise. The love and care that he lavished on her helped him keep a brave face for Ma's sake. Nathan was crushed by the knowledge that whatever he might do, nothing could impede the arrival of death.

There were no shafts of light in the sky when Ma died an hour before dawn. Nathan left her sleeping peacefully and, as he went to the kitchen to make tea, Ma's body convulsed involuntarily, hungry for air. Nathan was barely out the door of the bedroom when Ma's death rattle called him back.

Nathan gazed at Ma, her wasted body still at last; the shadow of life reducing, as her soul escaped from the damp sheets, stained with her sweat, from her futile struggle with death. Above her open mouth, her worn teeth visible, moisture clung, and on her brow too; Nathan wanted to dry her lips and her forehead. He was not afraid of death; not at all; might happily have joined Ma in eternal light. He moved forward, reaching for his handkerchief, and tenderly dried Ma's face.

First, he called Mr. Monty who arrived within the hour having driven from his home, upset that he'd not been with Nathan at the end. Then Nathan called the District Nurse who'd grown fond of Ma. She came before Mr. Monty arrived, and Nathan asked her to prepare the corpse before he summoned the undertaker.

The Nurse washed Ma's remains and laid her out. Using cotton wool and long forceps, she packed the anus, and sealed the urinary tract. Ma was so wasted that there had been little emission of body waste after death, but out of respect for Ma, the Nurse was taking no chances. The packing of these critical orifices complete, she wrapped Ma in a plain white sheet.

Later that morning, the undertaker, Mr.Wright, fussed about the deathbed. "Do you have Mrs. Forrest's false teeth, Mr. Forrest?"

Suddenly, Nathan's grief turned to rage at Mr.Wright's harmless question; he was, after all, simply doing his job. But the unspoken assumption that Ma, like many of her generation, had neglected her health, and appearance, and lived with a mouthful of ill-fitting plastic teeth sullied her memory, and diminished her courageous struggle for life.

"Whit are ye talkin' about?" Nathan said. "Ma has her own teeth. For Christ's sake, take a look at her."

"Nathan," Mr. Monty said, his hand on Nathan's arm. "Let Mr.Wright do his work. We'll come back in when he's finished."

"Mr. Forrest, later, shall I remove Mrs. Forrest's remains to the Church?" The undertaker said.

"No. She's staying here. We'll go straight from Galt Place to the cemetery."

"Gentlemen, please let me attend to Mrs. Forrest's remains."

"Come on, Nathan, let's go into the kitchen," Mr. Monty said.

Nathan turned, Mr. Monty's hand on his shoulder. "Mr.Wright, make Ma nice."

The kitchen was a desolate ante-room where Nathan and Mr. Monty waited impatiently for the undertaker's summons. Nathan shuddered and gave in to sorrow and regret, wracked by harsh sobs. Mr. Monty blew his nose into a brilliant white handkerchief.

"I could do with a drink, Nathan. Is the Maker's Mark still here?"

Nathan got the bottle of whisky out and poured Mr. Monty a stiff shot. Mr. Monty took a sip and then swallowed the rest of it. "I know you don't drink, Nathan, but you look as if you could do with something."

"No thanks; no drink." Nathan dried his eyes. "Sorry; Ah was thinking about all the things Ah should have told Ma, and didn't."

Mr. Monty held Nathan's shoulder. "You were a good son to Ma, Nathan. You've nothing to reproach yourself for."

Nathan kept back his grief and nodded to Mr. Monty. He was relieved when Mr.Wright called them to the bedroom. "Mr. Forrest, Mr. Solomon; please come in."

Nathan and Mr. Monty saw that Mr.Wright and his assistant had positioned the coffin on trestles to the right of the bed. Their mood was sombre, the drawn blinds on the windows, signalling a death in the Forrest house. The undertaker's artistry was hidden from Nathan and Mr. Monty: Mr.Wright had used his skills to bring Ma to an approximation of how she'd looked in life. The mortician's artifice blotted out the ravages of cancer on Ma's face. Ma in repose, and Nathan and Mr. Monty exhaled sharply, to expel the heavy odour from tiny scented sacks secreted in the coffin, camouflaging the creeping stench of rot and decay. Mr.Wright had worked carefully; he knew that Nathan's distress and sorrow at losing his Grandmother might erupt in another outburst of rage and criticism if any details of her appearance were wrong.

Ma looked well in death and at her rest. Nathan stood closer and rested his open hand on Ma's brow, the first of several farewells; a shock rushed through him as his palm and fingers recorded the chill of death on her flesh, chasing the last heat of life from his beloved Grandmother. He bit his lower lip and stifled tears and grief. Shards of emotional consolation nicked him when he saw Ma's reddened lips and the fullness of her cheeks. Ma looked better now; she had shaken off cancer's relentless attacks that reduced her body to a pain wracked wasted husk. He smiled briefly, seeing that her hair was parted correctly, as in life, a right of centre parting and he nodded approvingly as he felt the quality of the Last Shirt and the fine material of the veil, folded back to show her face. Nathan glanced at the Missal tucked under Ma's chin to keep her mouth from gaping; a discreet trick, a Holy conceit kinder than the clamps that closed the jaws of non-Catholic dead.

"Thank you, Mr.Wright. Ma looks very well."

"Yes she does, Mr.Wright. Thank you," Mr. Monty said as he stood opposite Nathan and let his hand rest briefly on Ma's brow.

"I can arrange the interment for later tomorrow afternoon; or would you prefer a cremation?"

Nathan shook is head and looked at Mr. Monty, who considered the furnace a barbarous thing: he had no time for the incineration of the dead and a scattering of ashes; all right perhaps for those without roots, their ashes falling on turf, reflecting a peripatetic life, walked on by mourners tramping through an anonymous garden of remembrance. Ma had not been out of Scotland; she was a part of Westburn. He shuddered at the thought of Ma consumed by the flames of the gas oven.

"Ma would not have wanted that," Mr. Monty said.

"No." Nathan said. "That's not on; Ma'll rest in her grave beside my Grandfather and my Mother."

Nathan was consoled by the thought that Ma, James and Olive would be united in death. He seldom visited the graves now. In the early days, Ma had often taken him to the cemetery and he could see that tombstones and flowers, the sight of disconsolate Catholics praying at the graves of their loved ones the gruesome rituals of remembrance depressed her. After the War the visits dwindled to anniversaries and gradually stopped. James and Olive were remembered by Ma and Nathan in conversation, the unexpected swings of memory, and remained a part of their life.

"Very well," Mr. Wright said. "You're quite sure you don't want me to arrange for Mrs. Forrest's remains to go to the Church, this evening?"

"Ma's staying here," Nathan said. "There'll be prayers before we go to the cemetery. Mr. Monty will take care of things then, with your assistance, of course," Nathan said.

Nathan was dreading the night watch. Not that he feared ghosts, certainly not Ma's ghost should she appear to him; but he could not bear to leave Ma alone in her room. Mr. Monty understood this perfectly.

"You'll be sitting with Ma through the night, Nathan?"

"Yes."

"I'd like to keep you company; you wouldn't mind?"

"Oh no. Ah'd like if you did that; thanks Mr. Monty."

"We'll be her Shomrim," Mr. Monty said; "you and me, we'll guard Ma. We're the Watchers until she gets to the other side."

Mr. Monty remembered the one other time he was Shomrim when his sister died just after he got out of the Army. It was important to honour the body and not leave the deceased alone.

Though Ma was not Jewish, he felt she might need help making the crossing; the way to the other side was uncertain and though they would not see her, she would know they were present and, if Ma was troubled on the way, she could seek understanding from the Watchers.

That night was the longest of Nathan's life. But Mr. Monty's presence and his love made it bearable. "We Jews have a saying, Nathan: 'Wait for Hashem; be strong, and let your heart take courage; and only wait for Hashem'."

"Hashem; what's that?"

"A name for God; we don't mention His name directly, but there are alternatives."

"OK."

Mr. Monty suggested a formal start to the vigil. "Nathan, let's ask for Ma's forgiveness for the wrongs or misdeeds we might have done to her."

So they sat quietly; contrite for a few minutes, each occupied with his thoughts, and asked Ma for pardon. Neither of them had knowingly done her wrong, but they sought condonation for their sins of omission.

Mr. Monty was bereft, for with Ma's death he'd lost a dear friend and an important part of his life, already growing fainter. And he wanted to hand on something of that life so that Nathan might take it forward. They nursed their grief with the old stories of the days when the pawn business was new, the stand against that monstrous Priest, Reilly. And his love of Flora Nash; and of Dorothy, who was now a part of their story.

Both of them felt that Ma was still in life; subconsciously they denied the reality of her death, particularly when her profile caught the moonlight shining through the drawn blind, her face without pain, her skin tight and looking young in repose. But she was on her way to the other side; Ma was leaving. Nathan and Mr. Monty hoped that she heard them and was not yet too far away. In the silence filling the room, Nathan longed for a last sound of Ma's voice. And it was cold; to have warmed the room would have spread the stink of death and shattered their lingering conviction that Ma was still with them.

"Nathan, you know I'm the executor of Ma's estate?"

"Ma never said directly, but Ah supposed you'd be taking care of things."

There was little money in the bank, for Mr. Monty had encouraged Ma to make her savings in precious stones, gold and silver that he kept in his personal safe; it was not a fortune, but was the modest harvest of careful saving: a tiny exquisite emerald, more than a chip and quite brilliant, a few good, though small diamonds, ruby chips, amethysts and the like; stones that sometimes came his way in the trade. Since getting out of the Army, Nathan had made good money down the yard; there was the cash in hand from gigs; he always gave Ma a goodly sum each week. Ma, having known hard times in the Twenties and

Hungry Thirties, had managed the household cash carefully, gathering the small weekly surpluses, investing well.

"You know that Ma owned the house?"

"Ah wondered about that; the way she kept everything nice, and no one else here bothered much."

Mr. Monty had seen what was good for the Forrests: at his wits' end persuading Ma that buying the house was the right thing to do; he'd loaned her the money, without interest.

"Well, Nathan, first Ma was shy of buying property, but she was a good business woman. If you sell, it won't make you rich, but it'll be a tidy windfall. You can let and get income. Or, you might want to stay here. It's a solid building and Ma made it nice."

Nathan shook his head; Ma had been an astute pawnbroker, but he'd no idea that, with Mr. Monty's guidance, she'd planned and invested well, making their earnings work for his future.

"Look, Nathan, you've got cash in hand, not a fortune but a roughness; decide what you're going to do later; but you need to think about that."

Mr. Monty mourned, of course, but he thought the time right to lighten the gloom and persuade Nathan to consider where his life was heading.

"Are you thinking about going down the yard again; back to welding?"

"No; that's finished. Whatever happens, and right now Ah've no plans. Welding on the submarines is out; it's over."

Mr. Monty knew that Nathan might make living at music in Scotland; artistically it would be barren and financially insecure.

Nathan had a good friend in Leo, but there were no relatives now that Ma had died. Mr. Monty was Nathan's Godfather, loved him as a son and was bound to him.

He'd been nursing an option for Nathan, waiting for the right time to broach it; he was convinced that out of Ma's death there might well be something good for Nathan.

Two in the morning and they were fidgeting with cold. "Dorothy," Mr. Monty said. "No word?"

"Nothing; it's finished," Nathan said. "Ah suppose she's found her place at the University."

Nathan missed Dorothy, but sheltered behind anger about the way she'd left him and inveighed against her. "Ah'd never have done anything against her, but that night on the bus, after the Jazz Festival; Philomena losing the place, Ah got the blame; for Christ's sake."

"I'm sorry, Nathan. Dorothy was such a nice girl. I doubt she blamed you; isn't more likely she was jealous of Philomena?"

Jealousy was an emotion that Nathan had briefly considered might infect Dorothy; but she seemed to be so pure and innocent. Of course, she was ripe for Fate to shaft her and unleash her fury. "Jealous? Perhaps she was."

"Nathan, have you considered what Chris said, about going to America; and I've wondered myself about Canada; might you go there? I remember you telling me what those American musicians you met at the festival said about Vancouver."

"Ah've not thought about it. There was too much on my mind; too many things to be done."

Mr. Monty knew that if Nathan were going to devote a career to Jazz, he might just need an alternative source of income; after all, in Jazz there are always dry periods. Moreover, though Nathan had done well musically in Westburn and its environs, it could hardly have been described as an economic miracle. The good money earned at welding, apart from providing the necessities of life, had too, assisted his musical career. And yet, though providing a living, welding in a shipyard could hardly be thought of as the ideal job for a serious musician. The electric arc of the weld was hard on the eyes; and good sight was as much needed by a trumpet player as toughened lips, strong teeth, supple fingers, and a well-formed embrasure, all at risk in the dangerous conditions of the yard where physical injury was common place: falls, severed fingers, cracked heads, and the like. Surely, now at this crisis, Nathan might be ready to listen to one or two careful suggestions on how he might fruitfully change his life.

Mr. Monty thought he had the beginnings of an answer to Nathan's dilemmas, and that he might just be ready to listen to him. "You know, Nathan, that delightful weekend I spent here and you and Chris played for me; I talked about you getting better as a player."

Nathan did not reply at once, and Mr. Monty knew that he'd be thinking of Dorothy and how happy they were together, rather than considering his future as a trumpeter.

Mr. Monty did not want Nathan's gloom to deepen. "I was a wee bit tipsy that day; the meshuval wine and the Maker's Mark. I never meant to offend."

"That's all right, Mr. Monty. Ah wasn't offended, but that day, Ah didn't want a change; Ah just wanted things to stay that way." He laughed. "All changed now, of course; Ma's dead, Dorothy's gone. Life, Ah suppose."

Mr. Monty told Nathan about the cousin in Vancouver; a scholarly bachelor and like himself, a pawn broker; a tolerant, amusing man devoted to the Talmud and Cabalistic dabbling. His family had stayed briefly in Scotland before moving on to Canada.

"What do you think, Nathan; Vancouver, trying your hand at more serious Jazz than in Westburn? The pawn; it's a good business to have behind you in lean times."

"Ah like the sound of it. But he might not be interested in me joining the business."

"Well, he's about my age and might like a younger man coming in to assist him. You'll be able to put money into the pawn; make a commitment to the business. Shall I write to him and see how the land lies?"

"You think we'd get on?"

"You have to go and see; but yes, I think you'd like him. I remember him as a child, and I've met him since; he's very funny."

"Well, if you don't mind writing and find out what he thinks."

Nathan was comfortable about taking the first step. No harm in that; and he could always back out if he did not feel at ease with the arrangements proposed.

Nathan moved uneasily in his chair. He got up and lifted the bottom of the blind and looked into the street. He turned from the window and gazed at Ma's veiled face. He felt guilt talking enthusiastically about his future and Ma hardly cold in her coffin.

Mr. Monty rose and stood beside Nathan laying a reassuring hand on his shoulder. "It's all right, Nathan. Ma wouldn't mind us talking like this. She worried about you after she was gone."

A faint lighting of the dark; it would soon be dawn. There would be more visitors to the house come to pay their respects to Ma and offer regret to Nathan. Many would express a wish to see Ma in repose, and Nathan felt obliged to take each one to the bedroom and lift the veil covering Ma's face. Often he wept. Mr. Monty did not offer to help directly, knowing that Nathan felt it was his duty. He busied himself, answering the door and making tea. And there was the final ordeal of Ma's funeral to be got through in the afternoon.

Nathan and Mr. Monty welcomed neighbours and friends who came to the house to mourn Ma and to pray for the repose of her soul. Leo and his wife were there. Nathan, and Mr. Monty went to the bedroom for a final look at Ma's remains. They stood by the coffin. In a few minutes, the undertaker would screw her down, securing the coffin lid forever. Mr. Monty touched Ma's brow, bent over and kissed her forehead.

"I'll be back in a minute, Nathan."

Mr. Monty joined the mourners gathering in the house, leaving Nathan to say farewell to Ma. Nathan composed himself; it was hard, but easier as he inhaled the stench of decay.

It was time. He laid his open hand on Ma's forehead, bent forward and kissed her lips. "Good-bye, Ma."

Nathan went to the bedroom door and called on Mr. Monty and Mr.Wright to come in.

The screwing down complete, Nathan, Mr. Monty, and Mr. Wright waited as the mourners packed into the bed room and overspilled into the lobby. Nathan led them in prayer starting quietly, faltering at the solemnity of the de Profundis; then his voice strengthening as the words of the prayer, remembered from his school days, came to him.

"Out of the depths I have cried to Thee, O Lord: Lord
Hear my voice.
Let Thine ears be attentive to the voice of my
supplication…"

Nathan wavered, glad of the swelling voices of the mourners joining the prayer and carrying him on; but he gave way, as he mumbled,

"From the morning watch until night, let Israel hope in the Lord," recovering to pray again, … "let perpetual light shine upon her. May she rest in Peace."

The finality of the de Profundis pushed him down, far into despair, and he could no longer hold back his grief. Far away, Nathan heard Leo lead the mourners in The Sorrowful Mysteries: his familiar voice, and the old, trusted words of The Rosary, its ancient rhythms drew Nathan up from the abyss of inconsolable grief, away from darkness, and into the light, "Our Father … Hail Mary full of Grace … Glory be to the Father…

He murmured a prayer for himself. "Oh Sweet Jesus, Ah wish Dorothy was with me."

Nathan, Mr. Monty, and Leo, and three neighbours lifted the coffin, resting the polished wood on their shoulders. Underneath the coffin bearers linked arms and made a bridge. Nathan was glad of Mr. Monty's firm hand. They carried Ma's coffin to the hearse parked at the door and eased it over the flushed rollers and into the vehicle. Nathan glanced back at the house and felt its emptiness.

The streets were wet from the heavy rain that had fallen all morning. Dark clouds raced overhead, but Nathan saw little of the troubled sky or Westburn's black pavements as the convoy of mourners passed slowly through the streets to the cemetery; he was bracing himself for the trial of laying Ma to rest. Two buses were parked at the cemetery gates, and as the cortege slowed to walking pace to pass safely, he saw the two lines of men from the yard formed up, and recognized many of them. There must have been close to a hundred from the Black Squad. He knew that they'd not be paid for the absence.

"I like that, Nathan," Mr. Monty said. "It's a fine gesture."

"Yes. It's good; Ah didn't expect it, bein' out of the yard for a while."

The Black Squad formed a loose phalanx following behind the car carrying Nathan, Mr. Monty, Leo, and his wife. When the car slowed at a bend in the path, they heard the broken rhythm of their heavy boots skliffing and tramping on the gravel. Nathan was moved when he saw the fifty or sixty people waiting near the opened grave; he'd not foreseen it, expecting only a handful to attend. The mourners made their way to the graveside, and the undertaker's men laid Ma's coffin on rough planks covered with a thick baize cloth. Nathan half turned and gazed for a moment at the polished face of the grey granite gravestone; he read, Olive Forrest, 1915-1933, beloved daughter of James and Millicent Forrest, Mother of Nathan, RIP; James Forrest, 1890-1941, beloved husband of Millicent, father of Olive, and Grandfather of Nathan, RIP. In a few days, the stone mason would add

Ma's name. Nathan saw the dark green moss encrusted round the edges of the gravestone and shuddered.

Mr. Monty beckoned the mourners with open arms. "Our lives are as straw, mere chaff before the wind and the storm that carries us away." He let his words weigh on the small crowd. "I want to mark the life of Ma, Nathan's beloved Grandmother, a good woman, and a dear friend."

Mr. Monty reached into his overcoat pocket withdrawing a black velvet yarmulke and placed it on his head; he beckoned them strongly and the mourners gathered closer. "I shall say a prayer for Ma: The Kaddish. I ask you to join and help; and say 'Amen' when I call on you. Kaddish is the great prayer of my people. It is a most caring and respectful way to express our love for Ma; and to make certain that her soul is never forgotten."

At Mr. Monty's words, Nathan looked up and nodded vigorously, gazing around the mourners.

Kaddish, that solemn, beautiful prayer for the dead. Mr. Monty proposed it to Nathan, who'd agreed immediately. Ma was not Jewish, but he felt that Kaddish would honour her memory and the repose of her soul. Mr. Monty trusted God and believed He would be unworried that Ma was Gentile; that Kaddish would raise her soul to a higher level in Gan Eden, finding the spiritual reward of the righteous in the world to come. Ma, a good woman who'd stoically endured a hard life, would benefit from their celebration of G-d, He who governs the universe particularly for man, his favoured creature; and in Kaddish, Mr. Monty would ask for peace of mind for Nathan from the only One who can guarantee it. Kaddish made it possible to accept the paradox that our sole comfort when we lose a loved one, is that the One who created Ma in the first place had now gathered her soul to Himself.

The wind dropped to a whisper and Mr. Monty's voice carried across graves and the wet earth and gravel paths, surged through winter's sleep: piercing the sparse branches where dying leaves wavered before falling, his words resonating off somnambulant conifers, oak and plane trees, sent back to the mourners by the host of granite, marble, and sandstone monuments guarding the dead.

"Glorified and sanctified be God's great name throughout the world … May He establish His kingdom in your lifetime and during your days … May His great name be blessed forever and to all eternity…"

Mr. Monty calling on the Glory of God and His infinite mercy; the promise of eternal rest for Ma lifted Nathan's spirit and he wanted to escape from the presence of death and to be away from the sight of decay. The mourners' 'Amen', and say, Amen,' broke into his thoughts.

Nathan's sorrow vanished in a fountainhead of resolution, and he knew that wherever his bones were laid to rest, it would not be in the Necropolis of Westburn.

Mr. Wright read the names from a small list. Nathan stepped up to the head of Ma's coffin and took the first cord; he was followed by Mr. Monty who took the second cord. Leo picked up the third cord. The husband of the District Nurse accepted the fourth cord, and neighbours were called to their place beside the remaining four cords.

Mr.Wright stood a little apart at the foot of the coffin and raised his arms. "Gentlemen, together please."

Nathan felt the weight of the coffin as with both hands he drew the cord tight and Ma was raised from the baize; the grave diggers removed the baize and the planks and he looked down into the symmetrical hole in the wet black earth. Slowly they lowered Ma to her resting place. Mr. Wright raised his arms and lowered them gently, and Nathan heard the soft clunk of the cords as they fell in gentle disorder on the coffin. They stepped down from the graveside and Mr. Wright handed a spade to Nathan who dug it into the wet heap of soil piled by the grave and gently cast its contents into the grave. He handed the spade to Mr. Monty, and he too cast a spadeful of earth into the grave.

Nathan moved forward. "Thank you all for coming. Seeing everyone here has made a big difference. I invite all who can to come to the Old Hotel for refreshments."

Nathan and Mr. Monty stood apart from the grave, near the cars to receive the respects and handshakes of the mourners who came forward. Nathan had a last look at the grave, and already, the grave diggers were at their work.

Near the end of the line of mourners, he recognized the Shop Steward, Joe Bain, and when he came forward was glad of his firm hand. "Sorry for yer trouble, Nathan. How are ye gettin' on?"

"Ach, no' bad."

Nathan introduced Joe to Mr. Monty, and they shook hands. "Ah liked that prayer; very nice," Joe said.

"Thank you, Mr. Bain."

Joe withdrew his hand from Mr. Monty's and removed a thick envelope from his inside pocket and thrust it inside Nathan's overcoat. "The Boys hud a whip round; it'll help with expenses."

"That's great, Joe. Thanks very much."

"That shite, Horse Jones, he hud it in fur ye." Joe said. "He went efter ye because ye were great wi' his lassie. There wis talk in the yerd, Nathan. But he got wan in the eye the day, when Ah told him we're a' coming to the funeral. He wis bealin'."

Nathan tightened his grip on Joe's hand, and allowed himself a mirthless, bitter smile; bealin': Horse Jones' stricken by impotent fury, "Sod the fucker," he said. "Ah'm glad of that, Joe."

"Mr. Forrest?" Nathan turned to a well-dressed woman in her early sixties extending her hand. "I'm sorry for your trouble," she said. "We haven't met. I'm Margaret Henderson. Ma helped me over a difficult time many years ago. I've never forgotten."

In the past, probably in the Thirties, this respectable middle-class matron had hit the financial buffers; the pawn was her last refuge. "Thank you, Mrs. Henderson. You'll come to the Old Hotel?" Nathan said.

"Yes. Mr. Monty was great help too, and I'd like to meet him again."

Nathan saw a small compact man hanging back; a Pocket Hercules in a charcoal wool flat cap, well turned out in the tough guy Westburn fashion of two decades earlier: a navy suit, jacket with wide lapels, wide trousers hanging over well polished black shoes, the shirt collar with long points set off by a tightly knotted and spread tie. He had a pugilist's face; Foxy Dougan, champion bantamweight in the Army.

John Dougan, Foxy to the connoisseurs of the ring, for his craft, and sheer guts in the fight: a man who'd struggled hard to escape his past as a feared scrapper. "Mr. Monty, how are ye?"

"John Dougan, I'm glad to see you. You're looking well. Nathan, this is John Dougan, an old friend of Ma and myself."

They gave John Dougan a lift to the Old Hotel, and he squeezed on to the seat beside Nathan and Mr. Monty. He'd been jailed for three months after a fight, and though provoked, was found guilty of assault. When John Dougan was released from prison, he had no job and little prospect of getting one. Borrowing from the pawn had saved him; and later, Mr. Monty helped him find work. As they got out of the car at the Old Hotel, John Dougan laid a light restraining hand on Nathan's arm.

"Ah might have finished back in the jail; yer Grandmother and Mr. Monty, they did me a right good turn a few years ago. Ah've no' forgotten, son."

"That's kind of you, Mr. Dougan. Thank you."

"Never you mind the Mr. Dougan, Nathan. Jist you call me Foxy; everybody else does."

The refreshments at the Old Hotel over and Nathan was moved by the people who'd come, and by their kind words about Ma; it was a fitting end to the day. There had been a quiet purpose after all to Ma's life; and in her sphere of influence, the arena where her power worked, she had acted well, and good had come of it. Her life and her work with Mr. Monty had reached some hidden quarters of Westburn, and he was glad.

One evening not long after Ma's funeral; they talked again of Canada and pawnbroking, but soon moved to the music. Nathan told Mr. Monty about the trio Leo and himself might form with Pat Daly, a bass player; a painter from down the yard who'd emigrated to Canada soon after the War ended, and he'd got out of the Army. Pat had moved to the US within a couple of years of arriving in Canada making his living gigging; and migrating to house painting when gigs were scarce.

"You've heard him play, Nathan?"

"No; Ah've met him. Leo brought him up to the house when Ma was ill; he told me he's a terrific bassist and a great sight reader. We got on, and Ah'm dead keen."

Pat Daly was now in his late thirties and unmarried, a working man turned bohemian, a veteran of juggling a living from two worlds. He wasn't a star, didn't want to shine so brightly. He was a working jazz musician gleaning a living from the Jazz scene in the Bay area around Oakland and in the North East, Boston and New York being particular favourites.

"He's home for about three months; his first visit in ten years. He wants to keep his hand in and suggested forming a trio; Leo, me and himself; no drums."

"Well, I liked the way you and Chris played for me. You swung beautifully. I liked being so close to the music. The trio might be exciting."

Pat's idea put enormous demands on the bass; he'd provide an imaginative rhythmic platform for Nathan's horn and Leo's alto. He'd brought records from the US of the trio the tenor saxophonist and clarinettist, Jimmy Guiffre, had formed with bass and guitar.

"Jimmy Guiffre, Nathan? Why, he's wonderful; one of the Five Brothers. Played with Woody Herman and Shorty Rodgers. I've been meaning to get more of his records myself."

A few weeks after Ma's death the trio, finished with intense rehearsals, made its debut at The Club. They were encouraged by the size of the crowd as they set up. Not a large audience but a respectable number for a wintry Sunday evening, and the mood of heightened expectancy in that drab and chilly room cheered them. Nathan, Leo, and Pat had worked hard in a short time, establishing a deep and intuitive understanding that was just right for the flow of ideas and imaginative leaps to improvisation in their new stripped down approach to the music.

They began with 42nd Street, in memory of Ma who'd loved the song when Ruby Keeler sang it in the film. The trio's was a lively version, with sad interludes. Then Gotta Dance, a bouncing funky song, a vehicle for Leo's wild and carefree alto. It was followed immediately with Have You Met Miss Jones, that Nathan insisted on playing at brisk mid tempo and subtle nostalgic undertones. He used the lower registers of the Flugel Horn to explore the melody, but an aperient bitterness crept in, infesting his longing for Dorothy, and he tried to purge himself of her. Nathan stooped to taking the piss of their affair, when he blasted his way through the song, and was so much at odds with the tender singing to Dorothy of half-formed love that June night. And Leo, unwilling to indulge Nathan, was soon affected by the strong mood Nathan established, the mellow, beautiful mordant tone of the Flugel horn contrasted with the high, cutting sound of Leo's alto; and the trio swung without drums: Pat, eyes closed, left hand controlling the flow of the chords and notes, the fingers of the right hand a blurred acrobatic and elegant flight across the strings, the bass, a flexible anchor for the songs, created and strengthened the exorcism with his own bitter improvisations.

Nathan and Leo, two welders, and Pat, a house painter, working men; musicians with novel ideas about Jazz, and the courage to challenge conventions with intense and concentrated playing; not at all tender, but moving between hard melodic statements of concentrated brevity and bleak melancholy. Their ensembles and solos were imaginative: a fresh, potent synthesis of popular song and the sadness of the blues; perhaps a little self-indulgent, not po faced or solemn, nor over serious, but untamed. Nathan used circular breathing in his duets with Leo, the Couesnon Flugel Horn ideal for the creation of long beautiful tones. Their playing was an appeal to the acute and sensitive imagination, a small and ravishing sound in the house of the music; a divine chapel in the Church of Jazz.

Westburn Jazz lovers, a conservative body, struggled to assimilate or identify with this austere and beautiful music; they were unprepared, might never be ready for the jolts of new experience; they'd braved the wind and snow that Sunday night expecting a familiar sound of a regular bass line, the reassuring, steady thud of the bass drum in the right place and the light, crisp sizzle of the Hi Hat and cymbals. When the trio finished playing On The Sunny Side of The Street, they had rejected the music, trickling away, vanishing as rain water in hot sun.

After the four long numbers the audience had dwindled to Mr. Monty and a handful of individuals, excited that the trio was breaking new ground. But the general lack of appreciation depressed Nathan, Leo, and Pat.

"Last number?" Nathan said.

They played the Tina Lina, an unusual choice of song for a Jazz trio. Nathan had arranged it, transforming the mood from gaiety to a sombre mid tempo interpretation in 3/4 time, close to a danse macabre. Nathan remembered the Tina Lina from the Mario Lanza film, Toast of New Orleans. The deeper range of the flugel horn let Nathan reveal a hitherto-concealed sorrow in this love song. It was an exploration of the shadows, a penetration of the dark quarters of the song; the rhythms of the bass bridging the ruminative humours of Nathan's flugel horn and the piercing chills coming from Leo's alto. It was inspired playing; a bold performance, punctuated by the asymmetrical pattern of bebop. Mr. Monty appreciated what was going on; but the trio's finale irritated the last intoxicated conservative in the audience.

"Whit's wi the fuckin' Mario Lanza?" he said. "Yez used tae be good, but this is shite."

The music stopped and from the corner of his eye, Mr. Monty saw Leo unsling his alto and put it down. Nathan shook his head and let his arm drop and drained the spit from the flugel horn onto the floor. The bass player waited, his instrument resting on his left shoulder. In a moment, Leo might launch himself at the drunk.

Mr. Monty, straight and tall as in his soldierly youth, strode towards the drunk, taking him firmly by the shoulder. "I'm afraid you know little of Jazz. Leave now. If the alto player comes over, frankly, you've had it."

Fright at Mr. Monty's words forced the drunk to his feet and Mr. Monty pushed him out the Club door.

"Ah hate this fuckin' time of year," Nathan muttered as he dried off the Couesnon Flugel Horn and carefully packed it in the case. He locked up the Club and walked with Leo and Pat to the car. They manhandled the bass into the back and Leo laid the alto case on the back seat.

"Mr. Monty, take a lift with Leo and Pat. Ah'll walk back to Galt Place. Ah want to clear my head. Here's a key; I'll see you in the morning."

All the black days of December, especially that desolate week between Christmas and the New Year when daylight was faint, Nathan had been deeply fed up, had hoped to shake it off and lift the gloom at The Club that Sunday night, but after the poor reception at the trio's debut he felt worse and his gloom deepened. The recital was a defining moment: Westburn had rejected their Jazz.

Nathan watched Leo's old beat up Humber Estate disappear into flurries of dense snow. He glanced east along the deserted main street, frowning at the thick snow flashing white in the sodium street lights. "Fuck it. Ah should've taken the lift."

Nathan still mourned Ma's death, and her funeral had left wounds. He could do nothing to lessen his sorrow, and if he turned from that sea of pain, his conscience nagged him mercilessly about Dorothy. His recent try at exorcism had failed, and he loved only her: she was his first love; the love of his life. Nathan had long ago given up the Faith, and though he seldom acknowledged it, had absorbed the tenets of the Church, and drawn on them at Ma's funeral, but he felt that God was punishing him for debauched lovemaking and corrupting an innocent girl. Though God loved him, Nathan could not see it; if this mortal state were proof of His love, then it was unbearable, and Nathan cursed God for taking Ma and leaving him without Dorothy.

Even as the flurries of snow enveloped him, he was glad of the walk back to Galt Place, hoping that the activity would shake off his sinking mood. Nathan hurried through the empty streets of Westburn, hunched against the cold, wetted by damp snow, covering his hair in a white cap, gathering on his coat, a mottled shroud. He strengthened his grip on the Flugel Horn case and wondered if Hell might be preferable to Westburn on a Sunday night in December.

Nathan was repelled by his choleric face when he glanced at its reflection in a shopwindow. "This is fuckin' grim," he said.

Nathan was heading East towards the docks, and remembered that summer day. He had to pick himself up; for too long Nathan had wallowed in sorrow for himself; self pity had dragged him low and he suspected that Mr. Monty and Leo were growing impatient with his hang dog ways. He came to the place where the slowly healing scars of the blitz lay beneath a pristine carpet of snow and hit bottom. Nathan filled with that summer day when Dorothy and Mr. Monty first met. He was sad a while, but in his heart, knew that unless he turned to drink, he could fall no further. He must rise up now or lose his self respect, and the esteem of Leo and Mr. Monty. Nathan crossed Cathcart Street to gaze through the thick curtain of snow at the place where the wild summer garden had bloomed, and was ashamed by the depth of his self abasement.

Dorothy had said something that day about the untamed garden, and had dragged Nathan across to that tiny parcel of hard earth where feral blooms thrived, and gently tugged the Dahlia from the soil. The sensation of the pollen in his nose returned, and Nathan sneezed. "Don't you see; these gorgeous flowers are a sign of hope," she'd said.

Nathan felt feeble hope taking life, warming him. He turned his back on the memories of that summer day and the barren earth hidden by the snow and walked briskly up steep Provident Street to Galt Place.

Nathan picked himself up and fought hard to recover his sense of worth and self respect. It was difficult coping with the New Year celebrations and the old rituals he'd followed for good luck in the coming year; the private ceremonies loved by Ma and himself. For a short time, as this New Year approached, Nathan was captured by nostalgia and the happiness of the past: the good natured jostling crowd, Nathan an adept in search of good fortune, getting his foot on the horseshoe embedded at the centre of The Square as the bells of the Kirk chimed out the Old Year and rang in The New. Returning to Galt Place to first-foot the house, armed with charms to propitiate The Gods: a half-bottle, a piece of coal, and silver coin, strengthening the luck that came with his dark hair and sallow complexion. Ma wanted Nathan to be first across the threshold as the New Year began and she cried, as the memories crowded in on her reflections. She would give Nathan a wet kiss on the cheek and wish him a "Happy New Year, son," as she opened the door to let him into the house.

Ma's death had weakened Nathan's links with the past, threatening his sense of continuity with Westburn; now severance was close, and the slow dying of the old ways, people moving from the town centre, spreading out to the boundaries where the grim new housing schemes lay.

"What's the fuckin' point now?" Nathan said.

Nathan disappointed Leo when he said no to the invitation to his New Year party. He spent New Year's Eve alone with a frugal supper eaten with his fingers straight from the wrapping paper: deep fried, greasy mince pie, and soggy chips, salted to destruction and swimming in vinegar; Ma would have been appalled. Nathan whiled away an hour or so in half-hearted practice on the muted Bach. He was in bed asleep by ten o'clock.

Nathan was on the way up, but still fought to overcome sudden bouts of rage and days of vexation at the way Dorothy had left him; anger sometimes spilled over into his music.

Leo had arranged a good paying gig in Glasgow; a drunk pestered Nathan for a request, amusing his friends by shouting from the packed dance floor. "Hey, you wi' the trumpet; gi'e us Flamingo."

Encouraged by the friends' laughter, and egged on by their women, he came to the edge of the bandstand before the bouncers could stop him. "Hey Big Man, come on now; how about playin' Flamingo?"

Nathan vaulted off the stand and had the man by the lapels, was a hair's breadth from delivering a Westburn Kiss, putting the head on him. Leo dragged him off and tried to calm Nathan down, but not before the leader of the band rebuked Nathan. "Any more a' that an' you're out. You're lucky I'm not sacking you."

"Ye can shove it, Mate; right up yer fuckin' arse." Nathan said and walked off the job. Leo was furious.

"Nathan. Whit's wrong wi you? Ye'll have us blacklisted."

That incident was the lowest point after Ma's death and Nathan was disgusted with himself. He went to Leo's house to aplogise, promising to bring his volatile temper under control.

Grief at Ma's death waned, and he mastered the sudden rages; day by day he missed Dorothy less. Nathan was calmer. The yard and Horse Jones were behind him: he would never return there. Of course, he still loved Dorothy and wondered if he'd always love her. Sometimes it concerned him that the love for her might poison him, keeping him from other women. Nathan gave himself entirely to the music, practising daily for several hours; and he sought work as a musician.

The weeks passed, and to his surprise, he saw that the ingrained grime had vanished from his hands, leaving them soft and white; his finger nails crowned by white crescents. Nathan continued to study with Thomas Youngman and worked for the certificate.

Nathan, having learned to drive in the Army, bought an old car, a small vehicle, and travelled to far away engagements; he gigged at whatever came his way: casual dances in community halls, weddings, and dances in working men's clubs. He secured a prestigious weekly gig on alternate Friday and Saturday evenings at a Glasgow ballroom. Nathan had cheered up enough to congratulate himself when he was engaged for a week to play in the pit orchestra for a musical evening by a well-known female singer of popular Scottish songs. He was making a living.

There was a prestigious blow on Sunday afternoons at the Journalists' Club in Glasgow. It was not where a musician might turn up and expect to play; you had to be known as someone who could cope at once, and, in the first instance, invited to play there. A trombonist in the pit orchestra asked Nathan to come along.

Nathan had finished sitting in with the trombonist and an excellent pianist, and went to the bar for an orange juice. "Ah, so you're teetotal, Mr. Forrest?" A woman with an American twang said.

Nathan turned, and a good looking woman in her late twenties smiled. She had thick, black straight hair, in a well-cut Louise Brooks bob. She wore a blue gingham shirt and a grey skirt. He liked her pale complexion and blue eyes; but what he found attractive was her strong, classical nose.

But he was wary, almost rude; this was how his ill-starred affair with Dorothy began. "Do Ah know you?"

"You are Nathan Forrest, aren't you?"

"Yes; so?"

"Oh, for Heaven's sake, Mr. Forrest: don't be so damned stand-offish; I'm not trying to get off with you. I'd like you to come over to our table and meet my husband."

Nathan jerked his head in agreement and accompanied her to the table. Her name was Anna Woolfson, and she was a violinist in the SNO; a lover of Jazz; a walking encyclopaedia on Jazz violinists, and adored Joe Venutti, Juice Williams and Stuff Smith. She'd heard about Nathan from Thomas Youngman. Her husband, Dan, played the clarinet in the SNO.

"We like what you did with Have You Met Miss Jones," Dan said. "It was good."

"Thanks," Nathan said, shrugging.

"Bluesy; I liked that. Sentimental at times, as if you missed someone." Anna said. "Next time try it without the pathos."

"Is that right? Not my idea. The trombonist wanted to play it."

Anna suppressed the smile. She'd guessed shrewdly. Nathan's hard face was finer than eggshell, a fragile cover for unhealed emotional wounds that he could not hide when he played. Well, she'd knock that out of him. She swallowed the last of the small beer she was drinking, bent down and removed her violin from its case. "Do you know Blue Monk; can you play it, Mr. Forrest?"

"Ah know Blue Monk; and Ah can play it. Right now, if you want to; an' call me Nathan, OK?"

Nathan followed Anna as she strode onto the stage, her heels hammering the bare wood. The drummer and bassist waved to her and she gave a brisk nod of acknowledgement. She tuned her violin with the bass. Nathan nervously puffed warm breath down the mouth piece and fingered the valves of the Bach. Anna placed a large folded white handkerchief on her shoulder, resting the instrument on it, securing the violin under her chin as she moved closer to the microphone. She raised her bow and looked expectantly at Nathan.

It was the briefest introduction to Blue Monk, and Anna used it to drive her swinging, discordant improvisation into the distant recess of the tune where its mysteries were hidden from all but the most inspired players. The rhythm section swung unobtrusively, the bass periodically opening safe routes back to the melody. Anna stood close to the microphone, bowing vigorously, her eyes closed, and her strong nose dominating her face. She ignored the bassist's offerings of succour, confident of making her own pathways to the outer edges of melody and back to Blue Monk. The drummer shadowed Anna's violin with well timed sharp rolls on the left hand, shimmering play on hi hat and cymbals, and sparing use of the bass drum. Anna's resonating, swinging improvisations did not intimidate Nathan; he was no Jazz snow cake, but a powerful intuitive trumpeter. He shot piercing dissonant blasts that shattered against the waterfall of violin-sound; the fragments pricking Anna to sublime improvised excess. Nathan wanted Anna to know that he was around. Her solo almost done, Anna opened her eyes and shot a questioning look at Nathan.

He began cautiously, not straying far from the familiar theme of Blue Monk, Anna's remarks on being out of love, about sentiment, and pathos had stung. Almost at once she began raking Nathan with shrieking but complementing interventions, urging him to go beyond mere competent improvisation. She was frustrated at his conservatism, and that he might waste this chance to shine.

A pause; the bass and drums playing quietly, and he heard the angry snort amplified by the microphone, as Anna exhaled through her beautiful nose. She twice struck the open strings with the bow and jerked her head encouragingly; the look in her eyes flashing a signal: "What's keeping you?"

Nathan did not try to deplete Blue Monk; could anyone? He did not improvise to pass Anna; he was far from sure that he could do so, but several times as he soloed, Nathan reached the same high places that Anna had scaled. She beckoned, tugging him, then pushing him on until he led strongly, and then sent tantalizing showers of notes and chords, moving Nathan deeper into the music. The tension between them ebbed, and they handed a couple of choruses back and forth; the drums and bass brought them to a stop. There was a short ripple of applause.

Anna brought the violin down from her shoulder and removed the handkerchief; she dabbed the dampness from her forehead, grabbed his shoulder and propelled him back to the table where her husband waited. She gave him a cool look. "OK; next time let's play without the sentiment," and laughed happily.

Nathan shook his head. This Anna Woolfson was crazy; and already he wanted to play with her again. Jazz in the Westburn Club had never been so exhilarating.

"This place will be closing soon," Anna said. "What are you doing for dinner?"

"Back to Westburn. The car's outside. There's a pot of mince and potatoes. Ah'll heat it up."

"Aaargh, chopped beef; you can't eat that," Anna said. "You're like Dan; he'd be living out of cans and newspaper wrappings if I let him. Come back with us. I'm not sure what I'll make, but it's bound to be better than mince and potatoes. And you can give us a lift."

Nathan was content after the steak and chips and salad. He'd refused the wine that Anna and Dan had drunk. During the meal he told them about the band, his adoption of the Flugel Horn and the disaster of the trio, the gigs, the studies and the hours of practice.

"Ah surprised myself. Ah packed in the welding, and Ah'm making a living as a musician. It's not a fat living, but Ah'm surviving."

Anna was from Chicago and had met Dan when he was playing in the city. She liked Scotland. "I managed to get a job playing violin with the SNO. Dan and me, we do private gigs together. I'd like to go back home sometime. It's livelier music."

"Tom mentioned that you play the piano," Dan said.

"That's right. Ah've an old Kemble upright; picked it up second hand. Ah arranged the songs for the band. A few times Ah've played piano at gigs. Ah've sung a few times at gigs; ballads, that kind of thing, if somebody asked."

"Ah; so you're the man of all the talents," Anna said.

Nathan liked Anna and was attracted by her unconventional good looks, but he found her sense of humour abrasive. He stared at her. "You think Ah'm a street busker? Ah started playing the cornet when Ah was ten. How long've you been playing?"

"Long enough,"Anna said.

Nathan cut across Anna before she could say anything else. "Ah had good teachers in the silver band; and in the Army the musicians knew what they're about. Ah know my job."

"I want to show you something of Anna's," Dan said, getting up from his chair, before Anna could retaliate.

He took Nathan to a large sitting room and Anna followed them. "Try it," Dan said.

Nathan admired the beautiful Pleyel baby grand; let his hand hover above the polished rosewood. He lifted the lid to expose the rich black and ivory keys. "Gorgeous. Ah've never played a grand piano."

"Do play something, Nathan," Anna said, forcing herself to be pleasant.

Dan placed sheet music on the stand: Vincent Youman's Tea for Two. "Nice song; from No, No, Nanette," Nathan said.

"Please sing a few bars, Nathan," Anna said.

Nathan smiled, anxious now to avoid a row. "OK."

Nathan sang a swinging version, improvised a little, and finished on a conciliatory note, "Can't you see how happy we can be."

They had a proposition for Nathan: how would he like to work with them? Not strictly Jazz, but popular songs played for private audiences; Baptisms, parties, Bar Mitzvahs; that kind of thing. Anna's violin, Dan's clarinet, and Nathan's horn suggested a full sound; and as the three of them played the piano, there was the scope for diverse trio combinations.

"The money is pretty fair; our clients are flush," Dan said.

Chapter Seven

"I've had a letter and a phone call from my cousin in Vancouver," Mr. Monty said.

"Is something wrong?" Nathan said, worried now that perhaps the cousin was backing out of the arrangements and that he'd be stuck in Westburn.

Mr. Monty's cousin wished to make a lengthy journey to Israel; he was thinking of retiring there. He had two questions for Mr. Monty: would he consider managing the business while he was away and once Nathan was settled in. And in the longer term, how would he feel about taking over the business and settling in Vancouver?

"I wouldn't want you to feel crowded, Nathan. What do you think? We'd be partners."

At sixty-three Mr. Monty, isolated in an affluent Glasgow suburb, dreaded the prospect of loneliness: he had no family left in Scotland and when Ma died a strong link with his past was broken. Mr. Monty found consolation in Nathan's company and was pleased that they got on so well, and though he had encouraged Nathan to emigrate to Vancouver, he was not looking forward to Nathan leaving. These few months since Ma's death, he'd subtly shifted from avuncular, respected mentor to a closer fatherly relationship with his godson.

"That's good news, Mr. Monty."

"You wouldn't mind my being there, Nathan?"

"Of course not."

"Then it's settled. I'll wind up things here and follow you to Vancouver a few months later." He rubbed his hands vigorously. "I'm looking forward to working in the business again."

But Nathan wasn't relishing his farewells. He'd decided to bear the expense of flying to Vancouver. Leaving Westburn by ship, the sentence of a week long voyage to Montreal, confined to a small place among strangers with no opportunity of relief, punished by the bittersweet pain of exile; it was no way to start a new life. Sailing away would be an unsatisfactory end to his love-hate attachment to Westburn: he imagined home fading behind the white wake of the liner, knew that he would love the town all the more, and his heart would ache when the sharp, familiar silhouette of the mountains faded to lumpen, anonymous formations as the ship surged forward to the open sea.

Nathan had been removing all but his most personal possessions from the house in Galt Place, wanting to arrive in Canada unburdened and free to begin again; he desired a clean break with the past. He'd discussed the sale of the house with Mr. Monty, who was happy to attend to it as he wound down his own affairs.

But breaking up Galt Place vexed Nathan. Getting rid of valued objects, worthless to anyone but himself, was upsetting, and he felt his world slipping away. Disposing of Ma's clothing to the Salvation Army made Nathan feel her spirit was leaving Galt Place and the life they'd made there. He could not bear giving away her personal treasures all at once, so he let them go gradually, and that left him with the sense that Ma was still near.

Some things he would keep until near the eve of his departure for Vancouver. Ma's leather bound Missal and ebony rosary beads would go to Leo's wife, a devout Catholic. The prized China to a neighbour who'd helped him care for Ma in the last weeks of her life. A few items of dinner silver he would sell to supplement his Vancouver bankroll. The sepia portrait in the silver frame that had been taken with Dorothy that Ma had liked so much caused more unexpected grief, and that irritated him, reminding Nathan how much he'd loved Dorothy and missed her still. One morning he picked it up determined to destroy it, but he could not.

"Fuck this. Too many memories." Nathan returned the silver frame to its place on Ma's dressing table and knew that he would take it with him to Vancouver.

Nathan unwrapped his Christening shawl and recalled that day when he gently wrapped it round Dorothy's shoulders. The gesture said that he loved her. The smooth texture of finest cashmere made him angry, and had the shawl not been the gift of Mr. Monty, an object that had belonged to his beloved sister, Nathan would have shredded it with his bare hands. He wrapped the shawl and laid it on a chair, unable now to make a decision.

That evening, Leo and Mr. Monty had invited Nathan to a dinner at a new restaurant, Franco's Grill the first establishment in Westburn to serve meals in the evening. They knew Franco from his occasional visits to The Club.

"Ah've been in once wi' the wife," Leo said.

Nathan looked around the restaurant, admiring the open tables, the intimate booths, and the photographs of Spezia and the Cinque Terra. "Jist as Ah decide tae leave; things start lookin' up in Westburn," Nathan said.

"How's the teachin' goin?" Leo said.

" Goin' OK wi' the Silver Band. Toner, the priest, tried to stop it, but the Band Master stymied him," Nathan said. "The Reverend complained Ah wisnae a practisin' Catholic. He wis sore at Ma's funeral; said Ah wis a heretic. The good news is that Ah've got a few private pupils as well."

"That's good. But Toner's a clown," Leo said. "He wis always a silly man."

"What about playing engagements?" Mr. Monty said.

"Good," Nathan said. "Ah take on anything."

Nathan was buoyant about his music: the dances, weddings; the few Jazz gigs in Glasgow. And the work with Anna and Dan had opened up a new world where he made good money playing and singing songs he loved. If hc was melancholic, thinking about Dorothy, he cheered himself up with thoughts of Vancouver and new opportunities in Jazz; and he was infected by Mr. Monty's excitement.

"Ah'll be stuck here masel' wi you two gone," Leo said. "Ah'd emigrate, but the wife'll no' hear of it," Leo said. "Try the wine, Nathan. Ah had it an' the wife liked it."

"No thanks, Leo. Ah'll have some of that fizzy water."

Leo was a first-class welder and if there was work down the Yard, he'd be employed. Nathan had few anxieties there. But he worried if Leo would cope, fearing that Leo's arena for playing Jazz would shrink; that he might give up playing. At best Leo would struggle to find musicians that shared his approach to the music and discover that performing was circumscribed by the musical tastes of Westburn's clubs and dance halls.

"Talk to the wife again, Leo," Nathan said. "Ah've had a couple of letters from Chris and he's thinking about coming up to Vancouver for a while, once we get settled; Leo, we could have a quintet."

"I'll have wine with you, Leo," Mr. Monty said. "And think again about Canada."

They enjoyed the fresh tastes, affirming their friendship by sharing the dishes of mussels, veal and sole. Afterwards, they were quiet and content, sipping small cups of strong coffee.

"Everything OK; the food all right?" Franco asked.

"Wonderful, Franco," Mr. Monty said.

Franco handed a shot glass of grappa to Leo and Mr. Monty, and another cup of coffee to Nathan. "Good; this is on the house. The grappa is for the digestion, and it'll heat you up for the walk home. It's a wee bit chilly out there."

Franco jabbed his thumb back to the open tables and shook his head. "Two weeks open, and tonight Ah get the first drunks. Jesus, Westburn."

Their eyes followed the direction of Franco's thumb to see a well-dressed couple. Loud, slurred, middle-class voices drew attention to them as they swayed over the food in the exaggerated motions of the well-oiled.

"Christ, it's Horse Jones," Leo said. "Ah meant tae tell ye: he got fired a couple of days ago; went on the batter an' came on the sub guttered. A director came on board and bagged him on the spot."

"Aye, an' that's his sister, the dreaded Zoë," Nathan said. "That's the gruesome twosome."

Leo led the way to the front desk, ready to settle the bill. Nathan was at his side, and Mr. Monty right behind, a good head above them. Horse Jones, the alcoholic turned public drunk, got out of his seat and stood in front of them, blocking the passage. Zoë was slumped in her seat, staring moodily at the remnants of her meal. Horse Jones ignored Leo and looked straight at Nathan. The sour smell of whisky on Jones' breath enveloped them.

"Forrest, the welder ... got rid of ... Pape less in the yard."

"Aye, an' wan less piss artist," Nathan said. "Welcome tae unemployment, Horse."

Leo tried to get between Nathan and Horse. He wanted to keep Nathan out of trouble that might delay or stop his emigration to Canada.

"It's OK, Leo, Ah'll handle him," Nathan said. "Start a fight in here big man, an' Ah'll injure ye permanently. Ye'll be in the Infirmary fur a month."

Horse Jones stared drunkenly at Nathan, "... touched Dorothy ... a lesson."

Zoë lurched backwards in her chair and sat up straight, her loud belch, the bark of a Bofors Gun, sending rounds of spit, and gobbets of spaghetti and meat sauce airborne, staining the front of her dress and landing on the tablecloth. "A Catholic after my niece, damned Jew … marrying a Christian…"

Mr. Monty's face was expressionless. He knew that there were hidden pockets of hatred for his people in Scotland, but this was the first time he'd come face to face with incoherent naked prejudice. He wondered how a man like Horse Jones could have reared a lovely girl like Dorothy. "Dear lady, do be quiet and persuade your brother to let us pass," Mr. Monty said.

Zoë slumped back in her chair, covering her mouth, stifling her protesting stomach. Horse had forgotten Nathan and stared at his sister.

Nathan turned to Zoë, "Shut it, ya wee shite"

Mr. Monty's hand gripped Nathan's shoulder. "Pay no attention to her, Nathan."

Suddenly, Horse Jones looked around and, dimly aware of the situation, forced himself to concentrate on Nathan "How dare you speak to my sister."

"You, fuckin' keep quiet."

Horse was a big man, but it could never be a square go with him paralytic, so Nathan would go easy on him. Nathan caught his tie and tightened it and trapped one arm with his free hand. He was chuffed by the grunts of pain when he drove his heel into Horse Jones' instep, immobilizing him. Nathan held Horse upright and backed him to the door, pinning him there. He was aware of Leo compelling Zoë to leave the table.

"Get off, get off me," Horse said, eyes rolling with fear and wild from drink. He struggled and tried to free his other arm pressed against the door, trying to land a blow on Nathan and releasing himself from the strangle hold.

Nathan again drove his heel into Horse's instep. "Be still, ya cunt, afore Ah gie ye a right doin'."

"Take whit yer owed, Franco," Leo said, handing him Zoë's bag.

"Come back here if yer lookin' fur the Clink," Nathan said. "An' cross me again an' Ah'll break yer fuckin' bones." Nathan ejected Horse Jones onto the street.

Leo pushed the noisy, protesting Zoë out the door to join her brother. "Get your hands off me," Zoë said.

"Thanks for takin' care of that pair of eejits," Franco said. "I'm sorry ye had the trouble in my restaurant. Meal's on the house. No, Leo, Ah'm no' takin' yer money; pay the next time yer in."

The four of them stood in the door of the restaurant and watched the brother limping and the sister lurching along the main street. Zoë retched, stopped and was sick in the gutter.

Nathan was in no doubt why Dorothy's father and Zoë hated him and that his presence had spoiled the glorious future they'd wanted for her, a world of university and middle-class security far ahead of his milieu of shipyards, welding and crumbling Galt Place; a working man with ambitions in Jazz. It had not mattered to Dorothy that they were from different worlds; and it had never concerned Ma. Nathan was not ashamed of Galt Place, his illegitimacy or his trade. He was proud of his musicianship and glad that he'd loved Dorothy better than any man could. Nathan thought about Dorothy being related to these two, knowing there was nothing he could do for her. And though he'd almost given Horse Jones a hiding, and might have struck Zoë, he could not escape a trace of pity for them. How sad for a talented brother and sister to sink so low.

"Good heavens, that woman is going to drive," Mr. Monty said. He watched Zoë struggle to open the driver's door of a car.

"That pair are dead drunk, they'll kill somebody," Franco said. "Ah'm callin' the police. Good night, Boys."

Nathan, Leo, and Mr. Monty walked along the main street towards Leo's house, for a nightcap. "Don't worry, Nathan, it's a cup of tea for you," Leo said.

A few minutes later they crossed Nicholson Street and, looking to the right, saw that Zoë's car had collided head-on with a police vehicle. Both cars appeared to be badly damaged. One policeman was sat on the ground nursing an injured arm. Zoë sat in the gutter sobbing and Horse Jones was crouched beside her, a second policeman standing over them. In the distance, they could hear the sirens of another police car coming to assist.

"Ah guess the police found them," Leo said.

"I'm afraid they asked for that," Mr. Monty said.

"Dead right, Mr. Monty," Nathan said.

"They're fur the high jump," Leo said. "Let's get away fae here, It's none o' our business."

A few weeks earlier a member of the Chamber of Commerce had approached Nathan; the Chamber was sponsoring a musical evening. Would they perform a selection from Gershwin? The proceeds to go to charity. Some musicians had waived their fee.

This man was a manager down the yard, doing his five minutes for the deserving poor, and had not acknowledged that he knew Nathan. "Not on, Mate," Nathan said. "If we do the job, we get paid. That's how we make a living."

The man from the Chamber suggested a modest sum. Nathan shot out a derisory laugh. "Double that, mister."

"That's expensive."

"Take it or leave it. That's the fee. Mebbe you should get a few amateurs."

Grudgingly the man agreed.

That Saturday night Anna and Dan had stayed at Galt Place after the Gershwin recital at Westburn Arts Guild, and later, playing after-hours jazz with some younger Westburn musicians. They'd slept on and Nathan prepared a late breakfast.

The trio's playing of the Gershwin selection had been well received; what a difference from that December night at the Club; but then Westburn was happy with the familiar. At the reception afterwards for Westburn's dignitaries and the musicians, Anna surprised the great and good, refusing wine, insisting on drinking small glasses of beer; rather a lot of them. Afterwards, Leo took them to the dingy place where younger musicians went for an after hours blow. Musically, it was a wild session, Anna sinking more small glasses of beer; and between numbers, flirting indiscriminately and outrageously, was a sensation.

Anna came into the kitchen, just out of bed, rubbing her eyes sleepily, wrapped in her white robe knotted carefully at the waist. Anna and Dan had slept in Ma's room. Nathan liked her tousled, unruly dark hair. She was barefoot, and her polished toe nails surprised him; he never understood why women painted their toe nails.

"Good afternoon, Anna."

"Orange juice, Nathan; for the love of God."

She drank off half a pint of orange juice. Nathan refilled her glass and she leant against the dresser sipping from it. "Did I misbehave?"

"The boys loved it; not so sure about their wives and girl-friends. You played brilliantly. Is Dan up?"

"He left a couple of hours ago. He has a pupil coming this afternoon."

"On a Sunday? I didn't hear him leaving."

"It's not our Sabbath, Nathan."

"Ah, sorry, I forgot. Did you sleep OK?"

"I slept well."

Anna reached into the folds of her dressing gown and brought out the sepia photograph, in the silver frame. "You don't mind, I brought this from the bedroom? The girl's Dorothy, isn't she?"

"No. I don't mind; and yes, that's Dorothy. It was her idea to have the picture taken in a studio with an old fashioned camera."

Anna had examined the photograph before coming into the kitchen. Now, she looked at it again and held it up so that Nathan saw it. Anna continued looking but Nathan's intense stare absorbed everything about the girl.

"You're crazy about her, aren't you?"

"Yes."

Nathan confirmed what Anna knew: that he was still mad for Dorothy. Such a young and lovely girl; so refined, genteel even, sitting in the photographer's chair, the hem of her dress covering her knees, her legs tilted to the left and pressed together. Anna could only guess how lucky Nathan must have felt enveloped in this girl's love for him. Nathan's face did not have a hard look. Now it was innocent, and infused with a caring look for Dorothy. Anna saw the confident way Nathan's hand rested on Dorothy's shoulder, looking down at her as she gazed up at him smiling. Anna felt an involuntary stab of the pain Nathan endured now that Dorothy had gone.

"Finished?' Anna said.

"Yes."

"Hanker for her?"

"Sometimes."

"Time to move on, Nathan."

Anna drank the last of her orange juice, rinsed the glass, and put it down on the draining board. She was attracted by the subtle changes in Nathan since she had begun playing with him: the mature demeanour, the intense, emotional playing and the brooding silences. She wanted to touch the white flashes in his dark hair; a delicate contrast with his sallow complexion.

"Byronic," she said spontaneously.

"What's that?"

"Oh, nothing. Tell me about Dorothy."

So he told her everything.

"She was jealous of Philomena, Nathan; the woman you buried. Poor Dorothy; all that pain of first love."

"Tough. Philomena was the past. But Dorothy wouldn't listen. She was sarky the last time I met her, and I was hard on her."

"Silly boy; and all your suffering too, at twenty-five."

"Good breakfast, Anna," Nathan said, breaking the silence.

"Yes, it was, even if I say so myself. Thoughtful of you to get the sirloin from the Kosher butcher. Very tasty with the eggs, tomatoes, and the potato scones. I like doing the odd fry up. When I saw the wrapper, I thought it was ham or bacon."

"I shopped for Ma; she was good at cooking Kosher for Mr. Monty."

By five o' clock rain had been falling for a couple of hours, settling quickly to a hard, steady deluge, cutting the late afternoon light. Listening to several of Nathan's records had not lightened the gloom.

"Glass rods," Anna said. "I hate that."

"Stay the night, then."

Asking Anna to stay another night was a long shot by Nathan to keep him from a lonely Sunday evening. She was good company, and he liked her. "Can't; there's something I need to do for Monday morning. I'll get the train. Anyway, Dan doesn't like it when I'm away overnight"

"Forget the train. I'll run you home around seven."

"OK."

"Looking forward to Vancouver?" Anna said.

"Quite a bit," Nathan said. "I'll be away from all the creeps that hate bastards, and there'll be no more of the Catholic-Protestant thing. It's funny, I decide to leave and suddenly I'm making good here at the music. Playing with you and Dan has been great. I've learned a lot. Well, anyway, I just wanted to say thanks, that's all."

"Well, we'll miss you in the trio. But Vancouver will be good for you. It's not New York, but musically you'll be stretched. But you're unhappy, aren't you? I can see it. Is it the girl?"

Nathan shrugged. Often, when he was very low, Nathan had wanted to talk more to Leo and Mr. Monty about Dorothy, but he was ill at ease talking to another man about her. Anyone else bringing up his broken affair with Dorothy risked a tongue lashing, but he was glad Anna had asked him; he trusted her. It was a trust that came from playing together. The intuitive under-standing they'd built up while performing was now touching his personal life.

"Yes. I waited a long time for her. I miss her a lot. She was never bothered that I'm a bastard, or a Catholic. And Ma loved her. They got on so well."

"I'm sorry, Nathan, I can see how awful it was when she left you like that. Can't you do anything; get in touch with her?"

"I wouldn't know where to start; her Old Man hates the sight of me, and so does her aunt. And I can't imagine her mother would want me around."

He'd already mentioned the scene in the restaurant to Anna at breakfast.

"Yes, I see what you mean. Try not to be bitter about it. I know that's difficult, but bitterness, it's corrosive; just eats you up. Try to remember how happy she made you. Be glad about that and forget the rest."

"Sure, Anna."

They were quiet for a few moments and Anna leant forward and touched Nathan's arm.

"I'm going to tell you something about myself, I'm not sure why, but I think it might help. Do shut me up if you get fed up with my talking. After I got my degree and started playing professionally, I wasn't very nice. In fact, I was a bit of a shit."

Men found Anna attractive, and she exploited it, seeing what she could get away with; she was by turns tender and cruel with her lovers.

"Sometimes I was nice to them, but more often I was heart-less. My body was a weapon, and I used it to hurt men. I wasn't making love: I was in some kind of insane struggle and I used muscle, bone, and spirit to win, to crush a man. Horrible I was."

When angry, Anna was in looks and a lover was hard put to resist her; and she loved a row driven by the rush of adrenalin, she pounced on her man: firing long bursts of crushing words.

"One man told me I was a dangerous cow and that I'd fucked him up. I don't think Dorothy had it in mind to injure you. She was jealous of Philomena and unthinkingly lashed out; she couldn't bear the thought of ever having shared you with anyone else. Now she doesn't know how to get herself off the hook. I bet she's hurting as much as you."

Anna's candour stunned Nathan.

"My trouble was I could see an erection in a man's eye, but I never let it go beyond that. I really was a bit of a rotter. I never let anyone look at me the way you look at Dorothy in that photograph." Anna held up her hand. "Don't stop me now, Nathan, let me finish. I never saw anyone the way that Dorothy saw you. I've seen the photograph and the way you looked at her; you can't deny it."

"You're right. It's true, but what the Hell: I can't do anything now. It's over."

"I know, Nathan, but in time you'll meet a nice Canadian girl. Don't play the fool with her, and make yourself unhappy."

Anna told Nathan that when she first met Dan she'd been by turns warm and then hard with him, but slowly he wooed her and stripped away her brash, flinty public face. She'd learned a lot about how he felt by playing with him.

Anna laughed but there was serenity in her voice. "I fell in love with him. I mean, Nathan, I went down hard. He made me so happy. That's why I came to Scotland; and it's why I stay."

There was a knock at the door. Anna was still in the house.

"Good; you have a visitor, now that I'm leaving. Don't worry, if it's important I'll get the late train," Anna said. "Answer the door. I'm going to get my bag and the fiddle."

Dorothy stood there in the pouring rain. "Can I come in?"

Nathan stared at Dorothy, taking in her dark grey woollen skirt hanging below a camel duffel coat. He hated duffel coats, a garment used by the Royal Navy and appropriated by students, worn with a long college scarf. Strands of wet hair clung to her forehead. She seemed to be standing there, isolated inside her heavy flat shoes, not really wearing them, and her slender girlishness that he loved was buried by that bloody duffel coat.

Then he remembered that first day she came to the house; how lovely and pretty she'd been in her red summer dress with the white fleur de lis motif, the girlish white sandals, clutching her white sun hat to her side. How lucky he felt that day; and glad to see her. But now she was so forlorn and he was aching at her distress. He wanted to lift her up and carry her into the house, but he remembered their last meeting outside the Old Kirk, and anger blotted out his surging affection.

"Why?" Nathan said.

"I just heard about Ma. I called Mr. Monty," Dorothy said, stifling a sob. "I'm so sorry."

Nathan gave a curt nod. He felt Dorothy's eyes on him. He knew he'd aged; she had aged him and he prayed that she would not dislike the patches of white in, what she used to tell him, was his lovely thick and dark short hair.

She was a sorry sight, and Nathan relented. "All right, all right, come in," Nathan said, standing aside to let Dorothy pass.

"Things are terrible at home," Dorothy said. "My father was sacked for his drinking. He was with Zoë when she crashed into a police car. They were both very drunk, and they're in police custody."

"I see," Nathan said.

After a row with her mother Dorothy had wandered the streets of Westburn, walking in the rain for several hours until she found the courage to come to Nathan's door.

They stood facing one another just inside the door; and where Dorothy had previously felt secure in the warmth of Nathan and Ma's welcome, the atmosphere now was frigid.

Nathan, weasel-like, delivered a low blow to maintain his hard face. "Why come to me, an Ol' Tim? You forgettin' the Teagues bugger their women?"

"l'm so sorry I said that to you," Dorothy said. " Nathan, I've no where to go .... I've no one else to turn to."

Anna had come out of Ma's old room with her things in time to hear this exchange. She recognized Dorothy from the photograph and was angered by Nathan's harsh voice and aggressive stance.

Dorothy, seeing Anna, assumed that Nathan belonged to her, and though she had no right to do so, was aggrieved and utterly weary; she leant against the wall. "I shouldn't have come," she said and turned and left.

Dorothy dragged her feet unsteadily into a curtain of rain shimmering in the street lights, head hung and shoulders slumped in defeat; she was crushed from seeing Anna with Nathan. As Dorothy vanished from Nathan's view, he knew that he should go after her and bring her back.

"Nathan, get her back into the house at once," Anna said. "That girl is badly upset about something."

"She can go to Hell." Nathan said.

But, Nathan didn't want Dorothy to go to Hell, he wanted her to stay; but he was too proud, too headstrong to go after her.

Just as his pride started collapsing and he was set to go into the downpour after Dorothy, Anna intervened, saving his face. "For Heaven's sake, Nathan; don't be such a damned fool. Why, she's lovely and she's so young."

Anna grabbed her umbrella, flying out the door, and into the rain. In five minutes she was back, and a sense of relief coursed through Nathan as Anna returned, guiding a hesitant Dorothy into the kitchen, having explained that she and her husband played professionally with Nathan.

"You're wet through. Let's get those wet clothes off and dry you out. Nathan, bank up the fire."

Nathan did so and put a clothes rack in place. Anna hung Dorothy's duffel coat, college scarf, and sweater on the rack. She looked at her damp blouse, the water dripping from her skirt and her sodden shoes.

"Can you go home later; have you a place to stay tonight?"

Dorothy shook her head, eyes averted. Anna made up her mind that if Nathan played the fool, then she'd stop him. Obviously, Dorothy must stay the night in Galt Place. "You can stay here," Anna said.

Nathan nodded, his resistance collapsing. He was ready to please Dorothy; she was in a bad way and he wanted to help her for he loved her. He was overcome by a desire to calm her and make her warm and safe.

"Nathan, stuff those shoes with newspaper," Anna said. "No, not at the fire, near it. Put them in a warm place. They need to be dry for the morning."

Anna turned to Dorothy and assured her that her outer clothing would be dried and ready. "Nathan will wash your blouse, your smalls and your stockings in his new washing machine; you'll iron them too, won't you Nathan?"

"Yes, yes," he said.

Anna continued hectoring Nathan and had him get night things, a dressing gown and heavy wool socks for Dorothy, and it made him warm and hopeful that Dorothy would be happy with him as he gathered things for her that had belonged to Ma.

"You need to get out of those wet clothes and into a hot bath," Anna said.

Anna took Dorothy to the bathroom and ran a bath. She sprinkled a good measure of relaxing salts into the water. "Hand me out your things. I have to leave for Glasgow. Sorry we're meeting like this; but at least we've met."

Anna handed Dorothy a card. "That's my address and phone number. Call if you need help."

"Thank you. You've been very kind," Dorothy said. "I don't deserve it."

"But you do; and Nathan knows you do."

Anna turned to Nathan as Dorothy closed the bathroom door. "Shame on you, Nathan Forrest, speaking like that." Anna grabbed Nathan's arm. "Nathan, she came to you when she had troubles. Don't let her down. For Heaven's sake be good to her."

"I'm glad you brought her back, Anna."

Nathan eased the poker into the fire and frowned as he heard it draw steadily, bright yellow flames springing up, sending waves of heat into the room. Dorothy was chilled and upset when she went to bathe. He turned as she came into the kitchen; now her face was flushed from bathing and the turban she'd fashioned from a towel suited her; he liked the patter of her bare feet on the lino. She was lovely.

"Thank you for letting me stay, Nathan."

"That's all right. Put on the thick socks or you'll get chilled."

They were silent from embarrassment of the circumstances drawing them together after a falling out that had lasted eight months, and never a word exchanged. One good thing: there was nothing to worry about from Horse Jones and Zoë; they were both in the clink. But Nathan had no idea what he would do about Dorothy.

"Would you like something to eat?" Nathan said, breaking the silence.

"Yes, thank you. Would toast and cheese be all right?"

Nathan moved the clothes rack back from the fire and handed Dorothy several slices of bread and the toasting fork. Dorothy toasted the bread at the fire and Nathan infused the tea. Then he buttered the toast, and laid a slice of sharp tasting cheddar on top of it for grilling. He set the tray on Dorothy's knee, and sat opposite her with his own tray. Nathan loved to watch Dorothy eat; she was so refined. He adored the delicate bites she took and the discreet way she chewed before swallowing her food.

"More tea?"

"Oh, yes please. I enjoyed that, Nathan. Thank you."

They sat quietly for several minutes, fussing with the cup and saucer, taking a sip of tea, pushing crumbs about the plates. They had so much to say but could not begin. He did not want to start with Ma's death and though he was glad to see her, he was not yet ready to tell her.

"Is Anna your girlfriend?" Dorothy said.

"No, she's not. I play in a trio with her and her husband. He had to leave early after a gig last night, to keep an appointment with a pupil."

Dorothy sat quietly again. She wanted to say something to him, but was having great difficulty speaking. Then the words came.

"I want to apologise to you. I'm so, so sorry, Nathan, for the way I behaved. It was horrible what I did to you. Oh, God I've never felt like that. I was so jealous of Philomena, and I gave into it and lashed out at you. I couldn't let it go. It was unforgivable."

"OK," Nathan said.

He was glad Dorothy had apologized and felt that he too should make amends. "I'm very sorry for what I said that day outside the Old Kirk. It was uncalled for."

Dorothy lifted her hand to Nathan, and he folded his hands round it, and felt her long and slender fingers curled at rest inside his cupped protective palms. It was a sign that she trusted him still, and he gently kneaded her palm and fingers, thankful when she pressed her fingers into his hands and erotically jolted as he gave the fine bones of her fingers lingering caresses.

"I'm so glad to see you, Dorothy. And I'm glad you came to me."

"Sit beside me, Nathan, please."

Nathan drew up the chair from the other side of the fireplace and sat close to Dorothy. He reached back to the clothes rack. "Your things are drying OK."

Nathan knew what was coming next and was dreading it. "Tell me about Ma, Nathan."

There was no easy way to tell her how Ma died, no words that would skirt round events. Nathan knew that Dorothy would take it hard when he told her. He wished that there was some way he could soften the blow of bad news.

"I'm so sorry to tell you like this. She died last November. She had stomach cancer."

"Oh God. Poor Ma; oh poor Ma. Was it bad?"

"Pretty bad."

Dorothy was very upset, and she wept for Ma, her great friend who'd lavished kindness on her and loved Dorothy for her own sake. And she wept for Nathan and a little for herself. Nathan knew he'd crack up if Dorothy's grief continued. He took Dorothy's arms and raised her from the chair, picked her up and sat down with her on his knees. She was so fragile and wonderful to hold, and he knew that he loved her.

"Oh Nathan, I didn't know, I didn't know that Ma was ill, or I would have come at once. Please believe me, I didn't know Ma had died. I'm so, so sorry."

"It's all right, Dorothy. Ma always liked you. She understood."

"Oh God; I wish I'd come to see Ma and now it's too late."

He sat with her and all his resentment vanished watching her grieve; he deeply regretted that he'd been so coarse when she came to the door. "Oh Sweet Jesus, but am I glad Anna was here. I'd have been just stupid enough to let her go."

Gradually Dorothy regained her composure.

"Dorothy, tell me what's happened to you."

"When my parents came back from Istanbul, I told them about us and about the row with Zoë. I said that I'd found rooms and that we'd stopped meeting."

"Did you tell them that she hit you and put you in the Infirmary?"

"Yes, I did."

Dorothy's parents were furious that she'd been seeing Nathan. Zoë, called to the house at Calle Crescent, was self-righteous and indignant. She cast herself as the injured guardian of a wayward girl whose hysterics, when told to stop seeing this welder, brought on a nose bleed, fainted and was injured. Zoë denied striking Dorothy.

"I told them to check with the hospital, and they'd find out about the bruise to my face."

"What did they say?"

"My parents dismissed everything I said. Both of them were incandescent with rage when they heard that I'd convalesced with you and Ma. They wouldn't accept that I was afraid to go back to Zoë's."

"My father said I was banished from the house and had to stay at the University; I wouldn't be allowed home until I apologized to Zoë. I refused."

"Did you tell them that she'd been drinking that night?"

"Yes, but they rejected that out of hand too."

"You mean you spent Christmas and New Year at the University when everyone was home on holiday?"

"Yes. They sent presents, and a card and I did too. But I couldn't go home."

"Jesus Christ."

"Nathan. Please don't swear, please, please, don't raise your voice. I feel that people have been shouting at me for days."

Nathan held her while she cried. He just could not grasp how a mother and a father could do that to their only daughter, and it hit him very hard that though they'd been apart when she suffered these horrors, Dorothy had fought for him, and he was sure that she loved him. They sat quietly, and he realized that Dorothy had been as lonely as himself at New Year.

"Dorothy, Dorothy, don't cry, don't cry. You over on the east coast and me down here on the west coast. You never gave up on me. You've been very brave."

"How was St. Andrews?" Nathan said.

"Not good. I found it hard to settle down. I was so unhappy I couldn't get it out of my head, the things my parents and Zoë said to me, or the way I'd behaved. Oh Nathan, jealousy; it's an illness. I couldn't study; and you have to work very hard there. I was a disappointment to my tutors. When I was in school I loved history and literature, but in St Andrews I was listless and bored. I tried to blame dull tutors, but that wasn't true. Most of them were very nice and helpful."

This log jam of lassitude and guilt was broken by a kindly, avuncular Episcopalian, a priest without a ministry who lectured on Philosophy. He sent for her.

"He was such a nice man, and he listened to me. I think he was shocked that I was banished from home. He advised me to come and see you and straighten things out. Otherwise, I'd never settle down to the hard work."

"I called Mr. Monty from St Andrews to find out how you were, and he told me about Ma. So I defied my father and when I came home to see you a few days ago, I walked into hellish row. My father said I was a wicked girl and again demanded that I apologise to Zoë. I was afraid, but very, very angry, Nathan. Oh God, drunkenness must run in my family. My mother said nothing as my father and Zoë were very rude about you, Ma and Mr. Monty."

"Zoë threatened to cuff me and I slapped her face, and it was a hard slap; just like the slap she gave me. I told her to shut up and to get out, or I'd call the police, but my father tried to get out of the chair, and I knew if he did he'd hit me. That's when I smashed the vase at his feet and that stopped him. Then they both left the house. God, Zoë must have driven her car. I was terrified, Nathan."

"Zoë deserved that slap." Nathan told Dorothy about the incident with her father and Zoë in Franco's Grill. "That must have been the day that you came home, Dorothy. He wanted a fight with me. I'm sorry Dorothy, but I stopped him and put him out of the restaurant. As we walked home we saw the crash with the police car."

"Zoë soiled the ambulance taking her to hospital to set her broken collar bone. The police were furious. And my father is in a secure ward drying out."

Nathan knew that a secure ward meant that Horse Jones was in Rocky Hollow, the alkies' name for the lock up where the Doodlum Drinkers, the Meths Merchants, the Jakies and the Aqua Velvet Men, aftershave guzzlers, in thrall to the DTs, inhabiting a quarter of self-induced hell with the Wee Green Men for company. He shuddered.

"Zoë put my father up to forcing you out of your job."

"He knew Ma had died. Many of my friends from the Black Squad took time off and came to the funeral. Your father was told by the Shop Steward."

Knowledge of her father's callousness upset Dorothy again, and Nathan dried her eyes with his handkerchief. Keeping Ma's death from Dorothy was a cruel and wounding touch. That pair of arseholes, making things worse when they were on the batter. He felt Dorothy's grief for Ma and her hurt as her family disintegrated. Falling in love with Nathan had brought her face to face with the realities of her father's life. Nathan was very proud of Dorothy's bravery, and she'd suffered cruelly for him.

"Oh God, Nathan, that's awful what he's done to us. He must be ill; sick from drink. Or he's just an evil man. Oh Nathan, I thank God that you don't drink."

After Dorothy and her mother returned home from the hospital and Rocky Hollow, they had a furious row. "She blamed me for my father's drunkenness; said I was common as dirt. I was raging at her. I told her that my father couldn't be cured of his alcoholism. Then I left. Nathan, he's been to dry out several times. I don't think he'll ever get on the wagon."

"What will he do now, Dorothy?"

"God knows. What's so awful is that he's a clever man and he could end up somewhere like Lagos, or Aden."

Lagos, Nigeria. Nathan had heard it called the 'White Man's Grave' by ex-seafarers down the yard. Aden, situated at the south end of the Red Sea, separated from Africa by the Bap el Mandep; an NCO he'd known in the Army told him it meant the "Gates of Hell."

"And Zoë?"

"Oh, she'll lose her job at school. She might have to move away from Westburn to find a teaching job."

"I see."

Nathan was relieved that Dorothy did not ask for more details of Ma's funeral. He would tell her later when they were both calmer. Right now, they'd both had enough of troubles.

Nathan told Dorothy about his life since leaving the yard. "I'm making a living as a musician. I've learned to adapt: I play just about anywhere and I'm teaching too. I promised myself I'd never go down the yard again."

"When I spoke to Mr. Monty, he said that you're both going to Vancouver."

"Yes."

The news that he was emigrating to Canada, and settling in Vancouver to make a new life in Jazz and pawnbroking shook Dorothy. It was simply too much to take in on top of the day's events.

Suddenly, Dorothy felt completely alone and she was very upset again. "I'm sorry, Nathan. I've no right to cry. I just hoped that we could be together again. It's my own fault. When are you leaving?"

"I'm just waiting on the final papers. It's all arranged. Mr. Monty will settle things here then he'll follow. Dorothy, have you any money?"

"Just a few pounds in an account at St Andrews. I suppose I can apply for a grant; and there's a legacy from my grandmother that's due when I'm twenty-one."

"How will you finish your studies?"

"I've not failed any exams, but I just scraped through at mid-term. I'd need to work awfully hard to pass first year."

"Dorothy, for God's sake don't throw it away. You're clever. You'll eat it if you put your mind to it. I'll help you if you need money."

"I'm going to sit the final exams. I think I can pass, then I'll see. I could become a bookseller."

"You could do that in Vancouver." Nathan said. The words just leapt out of him.

Dorothy looked away, too tired and drained by events to reply. Nathan knew that he wanted to be with her and had hoped that Dorothy might have been warm to his suggestion, but he could see that he'd made her nervous.

How could he stay in Scotland with Dorothy and keep his word to Mr. Monty? Beyond a firm intention that he'd find some way to help Dorothy move on from her present sea of troubles, and a growing wish that she would join him in Vancouver, Nathan had no idea what to do.

Talking about it could wait until tomorrow when he hoped she would be calmer after a night's rest and his head might be clear. Dorothy was drained; they'd both had enough for one day.

Nathan had forgotten the fire while they talked and, feeling a chill, turned to see that it had burnt low. He touched Dorothy's clothes; they were almost dry. He put a small bank on the fire to make sure they dried completely. Dorothy was drying her tears, upset again thinking about the horrors taking place at her family home.

"You're chilled," Nathan said, touching her shoulder. "Sit quiet a minute."

Nathan went to his bedroom and carefully removed the white cashmere shawl from its wrapping. He spread the shawl evenly over one forearm and caught one end in his free arm. He came back to the kitchen and stood in front of Dorothy, lifted the shawl over her head and wrapped it gently around her shoulders.

"That'll do it."

Dorothy raised a shoulder until the shawl touched the bottom of her cheek, bringing back all the happiness of the previous summer.

"I kept the shawl. It's yours. Whatever happens I want you to keep it," Nathan said.

"Thank you, Nathan. I'll have the shawl with me always."

Dorothy was staring through her drying clothes and into the dying flames of the fire. The sound of water running into the kettle brought her out of her reverie. "Nathan, what are you doing?"

"I was changing the sheets in Ma's room and heating water for a hot water bottle to warm the bed. You can sleep in Ma's room. You need to rest now. I don't want you falling ill on me."

"I don't want to sleep in Ma's room."

"All right; sleep in my room. I'll sleep in Ma's room. I'll change the sheets over."

"I'm not afraid to stay in Ma's room, Nathan; that's not what I meant. I want to stay with you."

Nathan worried that lying together might be their last act; and thereafter he'd be consigned to the dustbin of Dorothy's history, a player in the narrative of a foolish summer episode with a ruffian; a welder with musical ambitions. But that was unkind.

For Nathan, lying there in his bed with Dorothy was the affirmation of his love for her, this wonderful, lovely girl. To be sure, he regretted the heartache, but the bliss she'd brought him had taken him to a new place. He would not have missed her for all the world.

He held his beloved in his arms as she slept and worried about her. She had little money, and her legacy was three years away. If she'd let him, he'd take care of her, and get her away from this mess with her family. How could he live without her touch, the wonder of holding her, his hands tracing the contours of her slender, feminine body and the sweet joy of saying her name? But one thing he was sure of: if they parted now, they'd never meet again.

Nathan gently disengaged Dorothy from his embrace, and as she snored softly for a moment. He moved, and she opened her eyes to that shadow land between slumber and wakefulness and blindly kissed him and said that she loved him. Now he said it to her, and he hoped that she'd hear him.

"Dorothy, please listen. Come to Canada where you'll be safe and we'll be together."

It was the best that Nathan could offer. He could not disappoint Mr. Monty and bring him low; he would not shoot him down from the high plains of cheerful optimism he inhabited when thinking about going to Vancouver. He prayed that he was not asking too much of Dorothy, worried that she might feel brow beaten by him. He hoped that she'd heard what he said, then waited a minute or two for her breathing to return to the steady rhythm of rest and he turned into her.

Nathan had ironed Dorothy's clothes, and she was lovely wearing the duffel coat and college scarf. This morning she was not inhabiting her heavy flat shoes, but wearing them. They stood in the doorway of the house looking on to Galt Place.

"Thank you for polishing my shoes, Nathan."

"That's OK."

Dorothy held his hands and gently kneaded the palms with her thumbs. "Your hands, they're so soft and clean; a musician's hands."

She liked the way that Nathan had changed. He looked Bohemian and just a bit of a Romantic in the faded gold and slightly rumpled cord jacket he'd put on to go out. The daylight emphasized the streaks of white in his hair, lending him a quiet gravity. She touched the collar of his flannel shirt.

"It's so soft, and the faded jeans. Oh, the boots, I do like them."

"I asked Pat Daly to send them from Oakland. I suppose I was always a bit of a cowboy."

"I never thought that; not ever. You look nice; like a Jazz musician."

Nathan and Dorothy lingered in the doorway of the house. They liked what they saw in front of them. It was a fine April day with the promise of Spring in the sharp light and the clear air. Poor Westburn, barely recovered from the Hungry Thirties; battered and scarred by the Blitz, hanging on to shipbuilding, as an aged man clings to his last love. The old, tired grey town that Nathan hated and yet loved, was new again. The Municipal Buildings, the Town Kirk, the shabby old house with the Dutch gables and the red and honey sandstone buildings in the old commercial centre looked better in the change of season and from the cleansing of last night's rain. Even the cranes, engineered predators standing over the yards, seemed benign that morning.

They remembered that happy June day when they'd passed through the quarter on the way to the Old Quay. Nathan knew that the mood was fleeting, but in that moment he found hope for Westburn and for Dorothy and himself.

They walked the route taken by Ma's cortege, and Nathan told Dorothy of her last days and the funeral. About halfway to the cemetery they stopped at a florist and had the assistant make a bouquet of Spring Flowers; a simple arrangement of Iris, early tulips and, on a sudden impulse, they asked for a bloom or two of sweet-perfumed ivory Freesia. Nathan put his hand in his pocket, but Dorothy stopped him.

"Let me, Nathan."

They walked up Lord Nelson Street, the bouquet of Spring Flowers cradled in Nathan's free arm; they slowed down at the Old Kirk.

"I regret what I said here," Nathan said.

Dorothy's hand gripped Nathan's hand even more firmly. She looked up and smiled. "I offended you that day. I'm sorry for everything that I did."

The lovers quickened their step and swept past the Eye Infirmary, its red brick glowing in the sunshine. They strode briskly now, on past the Academy Grammar and the last proud Victorian tenements of Lord Nelson Street guarding the cross roads and the gates of the cemetery.

The stone mason had cleaned up the gravestone, removing the moss, and accumulated dirt. Ma's name caught Dorothy's eye; the bright gold letters contrasted with the fading glister of her husband and daughter's names. Nathan had kept the grave tidy, knowing that he was going to Canada and there would be no one to attend to it. They made a fan of the flowers and laid it on top of the grave at the mercy of the weather; a careless, loving gesture that would have pleased Ma.

The grave was on a mound, and Nathan and Dorothy stood there among clutches of swaying daffodils and narcissi planted in memory of loved ones. Ahead, through a sparse screen of budding trees, over the boundary wall, was the river, turning at the Tail O'The Bank, the gateway westwards to the sea.

They lifted their eyes to the hills. "It's very beautiful," Dorothy said. "I love the river and the mountains."

"Yes," Nathan said, his arm round her shoulder, feeling sad that she had not said what he wanted to hear, resigned that they must soon part and convinced he'd never see her again.

"Shall we miss all this, Nathan?"

"Yes; but there's sea views and mountains in Vancouver."

'We' Dorothy had said. 'We.' Nathan murmured; her voice was the nectar of Holy wine. And then, he was the old Nathan that she loved: passionate, charged with feeling that left him with few words, and he was glad that she'd come to him; glad that Dorothy's love for him had transcended her suffering; and now it would be all right. He held her, and she came to him. Nathan's face rested on her hair; her beautiful hair, and he kissed it.

"Oh Jesus, Dorothy; you're all my life in one breath."

"Darling Nathan; oh darling Nathan."

Nathan looked around the lairs, and the gravestones etched with the same family names, marking the passing generations; signs of deep rootedness in Westburn. They gazed at the lair where Nathan's family lay. Although he knew that he would loosen them, his roots were sunk there. He saw his mother's name, and his grandfather's name etched in faded gold letters and was sad that their faces were no longer as clear to him; then Ma's name, newly etched on the polished granite gravestone, the letters bright and her face still engraved in his memory. But Nathan was melancholy, knowing that in time, her name would grow faint on the stone and memory of her face would slip away from him.

The sun lighted Galt Place, and farther eastwards, the empty stocks of the once-flourishing yards, and the cranes, black silhouetted monuments to former glories; and down there too, invisible from the cemetery lay the sub. Nathan was loath to acknowledge it, but the yards had shaped him.

"Part of me will always belong here, Dorothy."

Nathan looked at Dorothy as she gazed east across Westburn and saw that she was close to tears, and he knew that she felt the weight of rejection by her mother and father. Dorothy had given up much for him. Nathan drew her closer and he loved her all the more in that moment.

"I don't want us to finish up here," Nathan said.

Dorothy nodded and moved closer to him. "I know. I want our bones to rest abroad. I never felt I belonged here, but now part of me will always be here too, Nathan, with you and Ma. So much sadness since last summer; but I've been so happy."

And they looked back to Westburn with affection, even love, but knew that they could not live there; and they felt the wind from Babylon, sending them westwards on a true course to Canada.

About The Author

Thank you for reading my novel. I write novels, the kind I'd read, and hope that my books attract readers who'll spread the word.

I've made a living as a seafarer, production planner, personnel manager, and university lecturer.

I like to write. When not writing I'm reading. Then finding time for Jazz, and travel with my wife, especially New York City.

Books by the Author

One Summer
The Last Hundred
The Music Room
Westburn Blues